Flames
of
Deceit

Carol Hutchens

DEDICATION

Dedicated to Larry for believing in me,
to Stan, Aaron, and Brandy for
technical assistance and scouting locations.
and to our first grandchild with great joy

ACKNOWLEDGMENTS

Special thanks to Ramseur Fire Chief Jay Ledwell
and his wife, Firefighter Emily Ledwell for answering my questions.
Any mistakes in the details are entirely my own.

Note:

There was a fire in the Chatham County Courthouse. Watching hours of news coverage of the destruction of the beautiful old building started the idea for this story.

All details, characters, and events in this book are fiction.

Flames
of
Deceit

List of Characters:

Mia Clark: a reporter, wants to find evidence to save her brother, but Jake Stone might prevent her from finding evidence and turn her over to police, and end her career.

Jake Stone: Judge and volunteer firefighter, lives by his own code and tries to protect others. When his courthouse goes up in flames, he is determined to catch the person responsible. Rescuing Mia Clark throws him off balance, helping her puts his career at risk.

Leigh Anne Saddler: a former model, tells reporters Mia's brother, a senator, paid her to end a pregnancy. But who really got her pregnant? And why is she framing the senator?

Phil Clark: Mia's brother, a senator up for re-election, claims the model is lying. Is he telling the truth about his relationship with the ex-model or trying to evade facts to protect his family and his political career?

Susan Clark: proud mother of the politician, wants her daughter Mia to find the truth, but she doesn't realize the risk to her daughter's life.

Chapter One

Whack!

A powerful blow landed in the middle of Mia Clark's back, sending her face first into the stale, cramped, and dark storage closet.

Bang!

The door slammed, smashing her body against the shelves, and trapping her in musty darkness filled with dust and who knew what else. Tension curled her insides. Memories flashed in her head.

Time whirled backward. She was four years old. Trapped in the dark.

She fought memories as panic sucked air from her lungs. Fear and desperation spurred her to action. Using all the strength she could muster, Mia shoved against the wood door.

Noise sounded from the other side of the door.

Hope flared in her chest. Had someone heard her efforts to escape and come to help? She opened her mouth to call out, but the pain in her back made her pause. What if the noise she heard had come from the same person who shoved her in this closet?

Who would do that? Why?

Fighting new panic, she pushed against the door, again and again.

Nothing.

She hadn't told anyone she was coming to the courthouse. In the newspaper article, Leigh Anne Saddler hadn't given any clue to her hiding place. What were the chances the person on the other side of the door had come up with the same idea? That meant someone had followed her.

Another thump rattled the other side of the door. Louder this time.

Mia tried to think.

How long would it take someone to search for her? Did she have enough air? Hands behind her back, she clawed at the wood door until her fingers hurt. Finally, her sanity returned. There were gaps under doors in buildings as old as this. The Courtney County Courthouse was over a hundred and thirty years old and she should have air to breathe.

Struggling for calm, she inhaled a deep breath and froze. Her nostrils prickled from the odor of smoke. Moisture dripped in her eyes. She could taste the acrid hint of something burning. Alarm zinged through her, renewing her panic.

She was breathing smoke.

New fears raced through her mind.

Old nightmares filled her head. Fear of being trapped alive in a coffin robbed her of reason. In the ink black closet, she could almost feel the motion of the coffin as it moved closer, closer to the flames and her death. Images played in her mind. Perspiration popped on her upper lip.

Anger. Regret. Frustration. And hundreds of other emotions stole the air from her lungs. *She couldn't die like this. She hadn't had a chance to prove herself, or buy a pair of red-soled shoes. She hadn't met her own Prince Charming.*

She had to get out of this building alive.

But the odor of smoke was stronger. Mia shoved at the door again. Determination added energy as she slammed her weight against the door repeatedly.

On the verge of passing out from fear and exertion, she put everything she had left into one last shove. By some miracle, the door moved. A sliver of light appeared along the opening. Renewed hope gave her another surge of energy, and she pushed on the door until she could squeeze her body out the opening.

Hands braced on her knees, as she gulped air, Mia noticed the pile of thick bound property maps stacked in front of the door. *Who wanted her dead? Why?*

Staring through thick smoke, she became aware of the footsteps trampling overhead and realized the blaze was coming from the roof. Shouts and sirens joined the roar of the fire and added to her need to escape. Feeling her way to the hall, she dropped to her knees and crawled toward the stairs.

Smoke wrapped around her, stealing air from her lungs. New danger threatened her safety. If firefighters found her in the building, they would think she had set the blaze. *She wanted to clear her brother and the family name, not make matters worse.*

Filled with a renewed desperation, she pushed forward. Suddenly a voice shouted from the floor above, "All clear, on this floor."

No. Please. I'm still in the building. The words screamed in her head, but fear of discovery kept her lips clamped shut. How could she explain her presence? *My mother made me do it?*

Keep focused. Keep alert. Or you will die.

Did this fire prove Leigh Anne had hidden evidence in the building? Who, other than the ex-model, wanted to ruin her brother? Staring ahead, trying to see through the wall of smoke, she crawled forward and struggled to remain calm. But the presence of the unseen pursuer hung over her like a dark shadow. The person who shoved her in the closet could be two feet away and she wouldn't see a thing.

And they wanted her dead.

Out of the haze slowing her brain, she recalled the dead animal on her doorstep Saturday morning, and finding all four tires on her car flat at the same time. Angered by what those events and the locked closet door implied, she was determined to reach the stairs and get out of this building. She needed her contacts in the newsroom to find answers.

Feet thundered overhead. Crackling and snapping sounds from the fire added to the roar in her head. She coughed as more smoke filled her lungs.

Out of the gray smoke heavy air, one thought filled her head.

This was not a game. If she didn't get out of this building soon, she would die.

⚙

Volunteer firefighter, Judge Jake Stone, tripped over the pile of dark rags at the top of the stairs as he made his way through the smoke filled second floor. The fire in the clock tower on the roof had escalated. The burning sensation in his gut flared just as hot. He wanted to get his hands on the person who started this fire...

The black form at his feet, moved. Jake bent down for a closer look. This was not a pile of rubbish. It was a woman with feminine curves and smut stained cheeks. Red streaked blue eyes stared back at him from a soot smeared face when he shook her shoulder. Her voice sounded gruff from breathing too much smoke. "Am I dead?"

"Not on my watch." Jake removed his air mask and put it to her face. Firefighters had called '*clear*'. Why was she still in the building? He had checked the upper floor judges' chambers himself.

Suspecting he might have the person responsible for the fire teased his brain, but he thrust the idea aside. Guilty or not, he wouldn't allow this woman to come to harm if he could help it. He knew the pain of loss too well after losing Sara.

But facts stared him in the face. Why would a building withstanding attacks from nature for a hundred and thirty years, suddenly go up in flames, unless his suspicions were correct? This blaze was an act of arson.

That idea offended him on a personal level. This courthouse was more than a building. It was his courthouse. A symbol. School kids came to the museum downstairs for class field trips. Area residents took pride in the building standing guard over the county seat for so long.

Now, the roof was on fire. Men doing repairs on the upper floors hadn't noticed anything before smoke alerted them to the blaze. Had someone deliberately tried to burn the building?

He intended to find out who and why. Many events in his life had occurred on one side of the bench or the other, in this courthouse. Today he was acting as a volunteer firefighter, and trying to save the structure, but his professional life as a judge revolved around this building. He took any attempt to destroy the building as personal threat to law and order.

The woman leaning against his arm struggled upright. Jake leaned closer. "Can you hear me?"

Her gaze found him through the curtain of smoke. "A-are you real?"

"The roof is on fire. We need to clear the building."

"Don't turn me in to the police. Please." She grabbed hold of his turnout jacket in both fists and pulled him close as she said. "I didn't set the fire, but I know who did."

Heart pounding, he stared into blue eyes brimming with tears from the smoke. For a second, he forgot they were inside a burning building, forgot it was his fault he had lost Sara, or that this woman staring so earnestly at him could be an arsonist.

In that instant, something happened to him. Longings he had thought dead for six years twisted his gut. Awareness went zinging through his brain.

Normally, he considered himself a good judge of character. His position as a judge demanded he be, but with smoke filling the building that symbolized all he believed in, his reaction to this unknown woman in his arms left him with doubts.

"Why are you here?" Questions raced through his head. Heat simmered inside him, ready to explode like the blaze on the roof.

"Please." Her eyes searched his face with a plea that would pull a response from any red-blooded man. He forgot he was a judge as he heard her voice rattle like dry paper. "Help me, please. No police."

His training took control, leaving him no time to wonder why his instincts had steered him off track for the past few seconds. It was his job as a firefighter to get her out of this building alive. "Can you walk?"

She nodded and stumbled to her feet.

Did he dare listen to her pleas?

Motioning for her to follow, he started down the stairs. Should he follow his instincts and listen to her plea for help or allow his duty as a judge to take charge? The answer came from his gut and ripped through him, reminding him of the past.

After having his life ripped apart by the loss of his wife and child, *he lived by his own rules*.

He could help the woman and get answers to his questions about the fire at the same time. If she was innocent, turning her over to authorities would cause her unnecessary inconvenience and stress.

And if she wasn't?

He refused to believe his judgment could be that wrong. He lived to protect the innocent, and she claimed she was. Her presence in the burning building didn't make sense, but he would give her a chance to explain. Getting her out of the building undetected wouldn't be easy, but he felt compelled to try. Until he found out what she knew, he would stick to her like spray foam on a blaze.

Helping her could endanger his career, but when he looked in her eyes, he felt alive for the first time since the night that changed his life forever. That night had ended his dreams.

From the second he encountered this woman's gaze, his heart had filled with hope. He was ready for renewed hope. He wanted to believe in life and love, again.

As a judge, he knew not to believe all claims of innocence. If she was guilty, he intended to find out why a woman looking like a dark haired angel with eyes the color of the sky, would do such a destructive thing.

The best way to get answers to his questions was to keep her close. After he found out what she knew, then he could turn her over to the proper officials. He glanced back to make sure she was following him and felt a stab of awareness straight to his heart. He had saved her life. She was his responsibility. He would keep her safe and find the answers he needed.

His reasoning made sense. The legal system he served was a tangle of red tape that would delay getting the answers he needed. Then it might be too late. If this woman knew who had started the fire, he needed to know who it was.

When they reached the first floor, smoke wasn't as thick. Jake checked the structure near the side exit. Confirming there wasn't any immediate risk from the fire on the roof, he turned to her. "Can you breathe okay?"

She gave a nod.

"Wait here," he motioned for her to sit in a clear spot on the floor about five feet from the door. "I'll be back in two minutes." With one last look to check she was okay, he stepped outside to join his unit. "Hey guys, I'm all right. Just need air."

"Jake, go get checked out. With all the area departments arriving to assist, we have more men than we can use. The ladder trucks from Moncure and Siler City units are taking over."

Jake shook his head, relieved he would have a chance to question the woman. "If you're sure, Chief. I'll check out.

Chapter Two

Mia leaned against the wall and listened as the firefighter spoke to someone outside the door. His deep voice sent shivers along her spine. Unexpected emotions slithered through her veins. Even if he had saved her life, she couldn't react to this man. Firefighters were her enemies until she proved she hadn't started this fire, but she hadn't found the evidence.

This firefighter believed she was the arsonist. She had seen the doubt in his eyes and felt his distrust as if he had spoken the words aloud. So why help her? Was this some elaborate trick to get her to confess to arson? She could imagine the headlines now, and a reporter having her name in the news broke all her editor's rules.

If she wanted to save her brother and her job, she had to get out of this building on her own. Shoving to her knees, she crawled toward the voices outside the door. Looking through thick waves of smoke, she watched as the group of yellow suited firefighters glanced back, and then turned away from the building.

Knowing she needed to escape and protect all she held dear, Mia eased out the door, and ducked behind one of the tall evergreen shrubs planted along side the building. The damp night air hung heavy with smoke as thick as San Francisco fog, but the eerie curtain saved her from detection as she scrambled from shrub to shrub.

When she reached the corner of the building, she bent double with the need to cough and gasped lungs full of air. Squinting into the dimness, she scanned the area, and realized she was upwind from the blaze. The smoke was thinner, the air easier to breath.

Now, if she could just find her car. She had parked on a side street, but which one. With the curtain of dense smoke, and all the people crowding the sidewalk to watch the blaze, she couldn't identify street corners. Time was running out for escape. Her firefighter would come back.

After saving her once, he wouldn't leave her in that building alone. When he couldn't find her, he would search for her, and she had no guarantee he wouldn't contact police. She needed to get out of sight. Mingling with the crowd seemed her best option.

Crouching, she ran across the courthouse lawn toward the nearest group of spectators pushing against the barricades. Once she eased through the group, she realized someone might ask about the soot covering her body, but so far, people were watching the flames shooting out the roof of the courthouse.

Anguished cries ripped through the crowd. She turned in time to watch flames shoot high in the dark sky, and quickly consume the clock tower on the roof. Moans sounded around her as a crackling roar sent black smoke spiraling upward.

Seconds later, the flaming tower collapsed.

Amid groans from people standing around her and the roaring blaze, Mia heard a helicopter. To the right of the billowing plumb of smoke, she spotted the craft hovering over the scene. The familiar logo of a news channel was visible and tension twisted her insides.

The enormity of the situation she had escaped hit a blow to her chest. Realization of how close she had come to dying made her feel faint. She leaned against the brick wall of the building behind her and forced in slow, smoke tinged breaths.

"Have a cup of water, hon, it'll make you'll feel better." A woman carrying a tray of paper cups, stopped beside Mia. "It's sad seeing that courthouse burn. I got married there, you know."

"Thank you." Mia said as she grabbed a cup of water as the woman shoved the tray toward her. She looked in the kind brown eyes filled with disappointment and loss. "I-it's so sad."

Gulping the water, she silently admitted her reasons were different from this woman's, but her words were sincere. Swallowed the refreshing liquid, she glanced back at the building. Ice clinked in her blood as she watched yellow suited firefighters search every direction. One firefighter came out the same door she had escaped from, and stopped. His head turned toward the crowd.

Feeling his gaze bore into the group, Mia swallowed a cough.

"Here, hon, have another cup." The woman pressed another cup of water in Mia's hand. "You look like you've been out here a-while. You must be parched." Reaching in a pocket of the apron around her waist, she pulled out a cloth napkin and offered it to Mia. "Use this to clean your face. The restaurant won't miss it."

Mia mumbled her thanks and wondered how she could get away from this warm-hearted woman, but like the answer to a prayer, so-meone in the crowd called the waitress, asking for water.

As the woman moved away, Mia looked toward the tall firefig-hter. He stood there, staring at the crowd, his head turning slowly as he checked each group. He was searching the crowd and she was his target.

How could she avoid him? Hiding behind the people in front of her, she dipped the napkin in the cup of water and scrubbed her face. When the water was gone, she pulled out the tie holding her hair at the back of her neck, and fluffed the long strands to change her appearance. Moving to the other side of the crowd, she headed down a side street.

Where had she left her car? With the early darkness of the Mar-ch evening and the cloud of smoke, the streets all looked the same, defeating her rush to get away. Really, there was no need to panic. She could have been staring at the wrong firefighter for all she kn-ew. Between the eerie light from the blaze and all the spotlights for news cameras, she could face her own brother, dressed as a fire-fighter and not recognize him.

With chills chasing along her limbs, she moved faster, searching frantically for her black Honda Accord. She had taken the exit off Hwy 64 to drive into town, but she couldn't remember how many different streets she had turned on after that.

Without her vehicle, she couldn't escape.

"Going somewhere, little firebird?"

Mia gasped as the firefighter's drawling voice sounded behind her. His hand touched her arm, sending ripples of awareness chas-ing along her nerves, quickly followed by guilt. Her thoughts sho-uld be about clearing Phil's name, not how her body reacted to this man's touch.

Turning to face him, intending to blurt any excuse to distract him so she could leave this town, she forced a clam tone. "Excuse me? Have we met?"

Any words she might have added, escaped her as she saw the firefighter without his goggles and hat. She forgot to breathe as his green eyes stared from a dark stained face. The heat of his gaze burned as intense as the fire behind them as his glance roamed her face. Even covered by soot, his firm jaw and chiseled lips were appealing.

Her firefighter was obviously a man to die for...
Wait.

She had almost died for one man today. Trying to clear her brother's name had proved more dangerous than she anticipated. Responding to this stranger, adding more complications to the situation would not be wise.

Ignoring the energy racing though her veins, she held the firefighter's steady gaze. If she had met this man in a less questionable situation, she would have enjoyed his attention, but he suspected her of being an arsonist. And she had no proof she wasn't. She had been in the wrong place at the worst possible time.

All she had gained for her efforts to clear her family name was the possibility of adding charges of arson to the offenses aimed at the Clark family. She had lost her integrity, risked her life and her career. For what? The risk of being thrown in jail and grilled by police?

Staring at this firefighter, who put his life on the line to save others everyday, made her realize she couldn't look into her brother's eyes and see the honor and dignity shining in this man's gaze.
Why was that?

Because Phil was a politician and they were famous for kissing babies and stealing their candy at the same time. Or did it go deeper? Phil came up short in comparison with the firefighter. This man's willingness to protect people from the dangers of fire earned her respect, but it also made him her enemy.

Anger flared inside her. Leigh Anne Saddler's claims to reporters had hurt more than Phil's political career. Mia had staked her reputation on her belief in her brother. She wouldn't back down now. But if this firefighter hadn't saved her, things could have ended differently. She owed him her life.

"I'm sorry, Mr. Fireman," Mia clutched a hand to her chest and fluttered her lashes as she looked up at him. "You scared me, jumping out of the dark like that. Did you put the fire out? Is that why you're walking the streets?"

"I'm here searching for a certain little firebird who is trying to escape." His words dripped charm, but the look in his eyes said he was serious.

"Firebird?" Mia arched her brow and tried a puzzled expression. "Is that the name of a car? I could use one about now. I can't remember where I parked. Would you help me look?"

The firefighter's laugh barked loud in the chilly night air as he took hold of her arm. "So you can run away again? I don't think so. You're coming with me."

"Excuse me, sir but I do not running around with stranger men." Mia tugged her arm.

His grip tightened. "My name is Jake Stone. I live and work in this town. Who are you?"

"Mia Clark." She angled her chin high and fought to keep her feet stuck to the sidewalk as she stared in his eyes. "How do I know I can trust you?"

"You're safe with me, Ms. Clark. Come quietly, or I'll skip the friendly questions and turn you over to the police."

Desperate to get away, Mia decided to try and reason with him. "Why would you turn me in to police?" She waved a hand toward the billowing smoke a block behind them. "I came to check damage from the fire. What's wrong with that?"

Mouth tilting at one corner, Jake Stone traced a line down her cheek and held his finger out for her to see the black stain. "You don't get this much soot by standing on the sidelines at a fire scene."

Resisting shivers caused by his touch, Mia tensed her body and glared. "I've been watching the fire for a while. And you're out of line, Mr. Fireman." She gave another tug on her arm. "Is this how you pick-up girls in Courtney County, because I'm not interested?"

A snort of disgust was his only response he propelled her back down the street, toward the crowds watching the fire.

"I want to find my car and go home." Mia dug her heels in and pulled back.

"Fine," he glanced down as she stumbled. "But I want answers, first."

"Who do you think you—"

"Hey Judge," a man crossing the street in front of them smirked as he called, "too bad your courtroom burned." Malicious laugher trailed after him as he disappeared in the dark.

"If he thinks destroying a courtroom will keep him out of jail," the man beside her snapped, tightening his grip on her arm, "he'd better not hold his breath."

The man's taunting words and Jake Stone's response hit Mia hard as a blow to her head. The facts came so fast her feet stuck to the sidewalk. Her blood chilled in the night air. Dread robbed her of breath as the blanket of smoke had done earlier. *This man was a judge?*

She'd been caught snooping around the courthouse by a judge.

"Judge?" Mia stared at Jake Stone as if he had suddenly grown an extra head. "Are you really a judge?"

"Rethinking your game plan, firebird?" The firefighter tugged on her arm and continued walking.

Marching her closer to…what? Suddenly, the overwhelming odor of smoke and memory of being trapped in that closet filled her with panic. She staggered. Her chest tightened. She couldn't breathe. The pungent odor of smoke filled her nostrils and robbed her of the will to breathe.

Her throat closed, her limbs stiffened, offering enough resistance so Jake stopped. He swung around, leaning down to peer into her face. "This pretense won't help you. I need answers, firebird."

Mia fanned a hand in front of her face. "I-I'm…not acting. I smelled smoke. It all came back. I-I can't breathe."

Placing a gentle hand at the back of her neck, Jake eased her head down, and spoke in a low tone, close to her ear. "Calm down. Take deep breaths."

The warmth of his hand distracted her from thoughts of the dark closet, of burning alive. After several long beats, her tension eased. Her lungs filled with air. "I'm okay, now."

She stood upright and took a couple steps, but head swimming, she slumped against the brick wall next to the sidewalk to keep from falling on her face. Being this close to Jake Stone was enough to make her dizzy without memories of the danger she had escaped. Who was he? What was different about him that allowed him past her usual reserve?

"Keep breathing deep. You should feel better in a minute."

Gulping air, she coughed and looked at him from moist eyes. "All I can taste is smoke. How do you do fight fires all the time?"

"Air tank helps," Jake shrugged. "You get used to it."

"I'll never forget that smell." Mia closed her eyes, pressed against the wall, and suppressed a shiver. *Or the sound of footsteps, following me.*

"You had a close call. Try to forget about it. Focus on breathing."

"Someone tried to kill me." Mia chewed on her bottom lip as she looked at him, but the instant she heard the words aloud, she wished she hadn't allowed them to escape. Lifting her chin, she watched his startled reaction. Surprise, then disbelief broke the stern composure he had maintained to this point.

He glanced around as if looking for the guilty person and stepped close. "What are you talking about? You said it was memories of the fire that scared you."

Mia flung out a hand. "I never want to smell smoke again, as long as I live." She blinked moisture from her eyes, hating the moment of weakness. Hated admitting her life might have ended already, if it hadn't been for this man. "It wasn't just fear of the fire. I could have run out of the building when I smelled smoke. Why do you think I was still in there?"

"That's one of the questions I need answered."

Mia pushed away from the wall's sturdy support. "Someone shoved me in a closet and blocked the door."

Jake Stone's green eyes bored into hers as if trying to see deep in her brain. "Are you trying to gain sympathy so I'll let you go?"

Arms crossed over her chest, Mia lifted her chin. "You tell me, Mr. Fireman. No, wait. Answer this. Do you think I stayed in that thick smoke by choice?"

"You're saying someone locked you in?"

Lips clinched to stop their trembling, she managed one jerk of her head as she stared in eyes probing hers for secrets. Finally, she managed a whisper. "Someone wants me dead."

⚘

"Come with me." Jake turned toward the crowd and tugged on

her arm with more strength than before. People mingled in the smoke heavy dimness. The smoke and spotlights from news crews created an eerie half day, half night, glow around them.

Jake pushed through the crowd, heading toward his black F-150 Ford pick-up parked on a side street in the next block. Why had he listened to Mia Clark's plea for help back there in the courthouse? *Why protect her?*

"Where are we going?"

Her voice stabbed his heart and gave him the answer. Something about Mia Clark melted the ice around his emotions.

Noticing the heat of her arm where his hand rested above her elbow, Jake realized he was in big trouble. For the first time since his wife died, his heart was taking charge of his brain. He was under the influence of an unknown female, and he didn't know why. Worse, he wasn't fighting against this strange reaction. Even his love for Sara hadn't left him feeling like this...

"To my truck." He stopped beside the tall black pick-up and opened the door behind the driver's seat. Half- lifting Mia into the back seat, he pushed her head down below the headrest and kept his tone aloof. "Stay out of sight unless you want to go to jail."

"I can't stay here," Her protest ended in a coughing fit. "I want to go home."

"Not without me, you don't." Jake cursed the urge to listen to her story. Mia Clark could be an arsonist. By listening to her plea for help, he had put his reputation and his career on the line. The yes-men on the town board would cheer his actions. He hadn't intended to give them knives to stab in his back.

His brain shouted for him to turn her over to authorities, but stronger emotions made him listen to her claims. He wanted to know why? Why now? Why notice this woman, after six years?

With a snort of disgust, he admitted he knew why. Mia Clark's voice sang along his nerves. Her blue eyes offered a path to heaven. And heaven help him, but he couldn't turn away. Living by his own rules was one thing, but responding to this stranger made him question all he believed was right. Teeth grinding, he ignored the warnings in his head.

"You have two options. You can stay in this truck or you can turn yourself in to police. Your choice. There are dozens of people around here who want to rip the person responsible for this fire to shreds. Take your chances."

"Please, believe me." Mia wiped her watering eyes with her sleeve. "I didn't start that fire." She stared at him with a fear-filled gaze. "Someone tried to kill me."

"Who are you, Mia Clark? What were you doing in the courthouse?" Jake held on to the doorframe and shucked off his turnout gear. So far, this day had been a disaster. Now he was making things worse by rescuing his prime suspect in an arson case. What was happening to him? Stepping out of the fire gear, he reached for the change of clothing he always kept in the truck, and pulled on a jacket and shoes.

Mia sat there, silently staring at him. His brow arched. "You either talk to me or the police."

Trying to ignore his strong chin and broad chest, Mia inhaled a deep shuddering breath. The smoke tinged air filling the truck made her cough, allowing her to stall. Hiding her identity seemed best, but Jake Stone's stern glare warned that she didn't have a lot of wiggle room.

If she wanted to stay out of jail, she needed to cooperate with him. Drawing in another deep breath, she faced him with all the defiance she could manage. He didn't have to know about her brother. Just surface details. "I'm a reporter."

Jake rolled his eyes and stood there, staring at her. His wide shoulders filled the door of the truck. One brow arched to his dark hair. Lips shaped perfect for kissing, lifted at one corner. A sneer? A grin? In the leather jacket his 'my way or the high-way' expression, reminded her of James Dean photos. Awareness almost sliced her in half. Even streaked with soot, Jake's straight nose and firm chin added strength to a face that made her pulse race.

Despite her body's traitorous reaction, she focused on his startling green eyes and accepted the fact that he was serious. He would turn her over to police. Sucking in a deep breath, she considered the options based on his reactions. Deciding to attack on a professional level, and keep her personal life private if she could, she tilted her chin and stared back.

"Don't say it. I get the message. People don't think much of reporters. Your reaction proves you are in agreement, but I'm telling the truth." She inhaled and then wheezed from breathing the smoke filled air. Covering her mouth with her wrist, she coughed. "My name is Mia Clark. I work for the Raleigh Reporter."

"I see," his lips barely moved, adding to his stony expression.

Faced with failure after one glance at him, she inhaled deeply and blurted the truth. "I'm trying to find evidence to clear my brother."

"In the courthouse? You aren't an officer of the court. You had no right to go through court records." Hands gripping the doorframe, he stared heavenward as if praying for patience.

Mia heard the doubt in his tone. Saw his brows arch, guessed his thoughts. Something like, *what have I done?*

If she didn't talk fast, she might have to call her mother for bail money. That wouldn't make her mother happy. Even worse, arrest reports made the law log on page two. Her editor would see the notice, have a temper explosion, and then fire her.

"I wasn't looking at court records." The doubt flaring in his eyes made her pause. Sighing loud as a sizzling blaze, she stared at him. "I attended the hearing last Friday. When I read the model's interview in the newspaper, my first thought was that Leigh Anne might have hidden something during that court session."

Jake's gaze flickered, reminding her, he was a judge. He had heard all the excuses. Even to her ears, her explanation seemed far-fetched, but that old saying, *truth is stranger than fiction,* was repeated often for a good reason.

For long seconds, he stared at her, doubt filling his gorgeous eyes. And they were yummy. Dark lashes outlined their green depth, making the color more brilliant.

"Why should I believe you, Mia Clark?"

His words echoed inside the truck with the cold warning of a man in control of his life. Jake Stone was all the things she wasn't, or she wouldn't be his captive. But she didn't have time to admire the man who tripped over her on the stairs. She needed help and Jake Stone impressed her. He had listened when she begged him not to call police. Still, she had to make sure. "How do I know I can trust you?"

"Likewise, Ms. Clark," he slurred her name as if doubting it was real, and waited for her reaction.

⚙

Jake didn't have any reason to trust her, but one look in her eyes showed him a woman in need, a woman searching for answers.

The past gnawed at his conscience. If he had listened six years ago, when the woman closest to his heart had asked questions, things might be different today.

He shook off memory of Sara asking him to stay home that weekend instead of going for a firefighter's training session. That was past. Mia Clark was his current problem. Being a reporter meant she was trouble. From the few minutes of talking to her, he would definitely stick with that opinion. *Big trouble.*

But something about Mia Clark jerked his bruised heart back to life after he'd hidden his emotions for so long. Despite the obvious questions racing around his head, he wanted to know why Mia made him feel things he had ignored all that time.

Why now?

He should be concentrating on damage from the fire instead of wondering how Mia Clark had slipped past the barriers shielding his heart. Everything about her indicated her guilt. Timing made her actions seem suspicious. Her clothing proved her desire to escape detection, but from what?

He could believe she was reporter dressed in black for investigative work on a story. By making that concession, he was giving her the benefit of doubt. She could still be an arsonist. But...

The fact was he found it hard to believe she had risked breaking the law to clear her brother. More likely, she was on the trail of her next big headline and didn't want to give clues away. But one question wouldn't leave his mind. Why had he listened to the pleas of a woman he had never met before now?

The courthouse behind him was burning. If Mia Clark hadn't set that fire, she might know who had. He had heard the panic in her voice. Until he questioned her further, he wouldn't know if he had used good judgment or fallen under the spell of her stubborn chin and sapphire colored eyes.

Listening to her could put the only thing that had kept him sane for the past six years on the line, his career. As a sitting judge, he needed to make the right decisions, but he kept asking the same question. Why had he listened Mia Clark's plea for help?

Chapter Three

Mia sighed as Jake slammed the rear door of the truck and closed her in the backseat. Struggling to shake the numbness from her sluggish limbs, she leaned forward as he climbed behind the wheel. "Where are we going?"

Jake glanced over his shoulder. "Stay down out of sight."

"You're leaving before the fire is out?" Mia didn't dare analyze her reaction to his deep voice. This wasn't the time for personal issues. Her efforts to clear Phil's name had backfired. All she had done so far was make things worse.

Jake Stone was a judge, for crying out-loud. The man spent his life enforcing the law and to make matters worse, he had rescued her. Would he understand why she had to find the truth about the ex-model's claims? Did he believe her? Could his influence as a judge have any affect Phil's chances at re-election?

She couldn't let things get that far. She had to convince Jake she was telling the truth. Goading him about leaving the scene of the fire wasn't the way. Sibling rivalry aside, normally she was nice to people she met. Why this sudden need to protect her deepest thoughts from Jake?

"Local units with ladder trucks took over the scene." Jake turned on the ignition. "There are still hot spots where the clock tower collapsed, but the building isn't a total loss."

"What about the courtroom on the second floor?" Regretting the words the second they left her mouth, she held her breath and waited. Had she revealed what had drawn her to the building? Jake Stone was smart. He already suspected she was up to something by her presence in the courthouse. Now, he could guess…

"With all the wood paneling and benches in the room, I doubt there's much left to save if the fire got that far."

She hit the back of his seat with a bunched fist. "I need a lift to my car."

Meeting her glare in the rearview mirror, he said. "You aren't going anywhere without me until I get answers."

"You can't hold me. You aren't a police officer. I want to go home." She shoved against the back of his seat with pent up frustration. "My bladder is about to explode. I didn't expect my errand to take this long."

"I could drop you by the police station." Jake checked for oncoming traffic and made a left turn. "Or you can go with me and answer questions."

"Can we stop for food? I'm starved."

"Fine, but don't try to get away,"

Mia rolled her eyes. "It's a little late for threats? I'm in your truck."

"Why were you really in the courthouse?"

Chewing on the inside of her lip, Mia looked out the side window and watched lights flash past. "I told you, I was trying to find evidence to clear my brother."

Jake met her glance in the rearview mirror.

Her face burned with heat. Did she have to explain everything? Why couldn't he just accept her word? "I already told you."

"You must really love your brother."

Was she crazy to trust this man? A firefighter and a local, he was probably a fan of the ex-model's? Maybe they had gone to school together. "It would help a lot if you'd let me pick up my car."

Silence except for the whining of truck tires on the asphalt surface.

Okay, she was in this too deep to expect to escape without complications, but how much should she tell him? He had connections with the police. Was that why he wasn't worried about turning her in? Could she be in the clutches of a mad man? Maybe he thought no one would miss her. "Where are we going? How do I know I can trust you?"

He glanced at her in the mirror. "Trust is running a little thin right now, wouldn't you say, Ms. Clark?"

Before she could act on the urge to jump out the door of the moving vehicle, he pulled the truck into a parking lot and stopped in front of an all night restaurant.

"We're here."

She scrambled out the rear door, unsure whether to dash for the restroom or freedom. Her stomach growled, making the decision. So she followed Jake to the door.

Their steps echoed in the empty restaurant as they walked toward the restrooms. Two employees leaned against the front counter, watching them. Jake nodded to the women, and urged Mia forward with his hand to her waist.

His firm touch on her lower back burned her skin and made her aware of his every move. Chills skated down her spine in contrast to the warmth of his touch. Heat pooled in her cheeks. In another time, another place, she would enjoy her reaction to his masterful touch. If only…

Jake stopped in front of the door marked Women. "Are you going to be here when I come out?"

Had he sensed her urge to run? Or did he think she was guilty and running was what guilty suspects did? Eyes glaring, she tossed her hair over her shoulder and forced steel into her voice. "Don't you think I would have run by now if I'd planned to?"

"You tried that already, firebird." The muscle along his jaw bulged as he turned away. "I'm going to wash up."

Her insides withering with reaction to his implications and her need to trust him. But reality distracted her. She groaned when she saw her reflection in the mirror. It was no wonder the employees stared when she and Jake walked in. Her attempts to wash off the soot with the cup of water and napkin had made things worse.

Several minutes later, after soaping and re-soaping her face and hands, she walked out of the restroom to face the man who had saved her life. Jake Stone had rescued her twice. First, when he'd gotten her out of that burning building, and again, when he hadn't turned her over to police. She owed him for her life and her self-respect.

Her mother and Phil would have a fit if she were arrested.

Worse, if her escapades had made the news, she would lose her job. She could hear her boss repeat his favorite phrase, *"News is what we report, not what we do".*

Sighing, she forced her attention to Jake Stone as she crossed the room. He had chosen a corner table, away from the front counter. With his face washed, his hair slicked back, he looked different. The black t-shirt hugging impressive muscles made him look younger than she had first thought. And stronger. More appealing.

She gulped back a wave of emotion. It wasn't just his voice that sent shivers racing through her limbs. Every nerve in her body vibrated at the sight of him, forcing her to fight to keep from becoming a fan. How could she help? With his appearance, Jake Stone should have his own firefighter of the year calendar.

Hands clenched at her sides, she covered the last few steps to the table. Jake glanced up as she approached. Her heart lurched. Lashes, dark as his hair, framed eyes glowing with green sparks. *Wow, he washed up good.*

Dropping into the chair opposite him, she picked up the menu.

"The eggs are good," His voice rumbled in the echoing silence of the empty restaurant.

"I'll just have something to drink." She slapped the menu on the table, refusing to look at the mouthwatering photos or admit to the gnawing in her stomach.

"You're hungry. I heard your stomach growl."

Chin angled high, she glared at him. "I left my purse in the car, okay."

Jake swore under his breath. "Order food, damn it, I'm starved and I don't like eating alone."

"Fine, I'll have pancakes since you asked so nicely." She turned her snarl into a smile as the waitress appeared at the table. "Oh, good, you brought coffee."

After filling their coffee cups, the woman took their orders and left.

Mia lifted her gaze to meet Jake's and forced a word past clenched teeth. "Thanks."

"Forget it. You're a cheap date."

Date!

Her heart thumped. Jake Stone looked like a man she would date in normal circumstances. From the second she laid eyes on him, she hadn't found a thing wrong with him. Except he was a judge, and that made him off-limits. She had crossed the line when she slipped past security to enter the courthouse. She needed to keep away from Jake.

"Now you want to tell me what's going on? And don't say your mother made you do it."

Okay, she had found a flaw. His annoying habit of jumping on a subject and not letting go, and using that courtroom tone made him less than perfect. "I don't—"

"No more lies to waste my time. Tell me what you were doing in that building or—"

"Lower your voice," she snapped through clenched teeth and glanced over her shoulder. Satisfied that no one had overheard, she leaned toward him. "This isn't about me, okay? Not one word of this can get back to reporters."

"You're a reporter. Or was that another lie?" His brows arched to his slicked back hair, and his deep green gaze bored into her. Finally, a noisy sigh escaped his lips, conceding defeat of their battling stares. "Sorry, go on."

She blinked, her mind filled with thoughts of those perfect lips. She wanted to... Leaning as far back as her chair allowed, she forced back the images playing in her head and struggled with the tension blocking her words. Should she tell him the truth, or try to conceal facts to protect Phil?

A glance at the rigid set of Jake's firm jaw told her she was out of choices. No more delays. If she wanted to avoid going to jail, it was time to tell him the whole truth. "A former model claims my brother paid her to terminate her pregnancy."

"Senator Phil Clark is your brother?"

Mia nodded. "He wants to stop the rumors. Protect his wife and children. "

Jake lifted a shoulder. "Nothing new about that situation, it's in the paper. That doesn't explain why you were in the courthouse."

"Here you go." The waitress arrived with loaded plates. "You been fighting the fire at the courthouse?"

Brow arched, Jake's gaze searched Mia's face before he turned to the woman and gave a nod.

Mia clenched her hands in her lap and stared at her plate.

"That's what I told Doris." She walked a few steps away and

turned back. "Eat all you want. It's on the house. We need more heroes like you."

Mia peeped through her lashes. With broad shoulders and good looks, Jake looked like a hero, but she didn't deserve the honor. "How long have you been a firefighter?"

He paused with the cup halfway to his lips. "Eat. Talk later."

In hungry firefighter's terms, later was defined as a ten-minute recess. Jake put his fork down on the empty plate and watched as she chewed the last bite of her pancakes.

"Stop looking at me like that. I'm telling the truth. Phil met her through a business contact, and refuted all Leigh Anne Saddler's claims at the hearing last Friday."

"She lied in my courtroom?"

"Yes." Mia wondered about that *my*. What did he mean? He hadn't been the presiding judge.

"You're talking about the case causing all the media hoop-la last week?" His sharp gaze bored into her.

Mia gave a nod and swallowed back the lump of pancakes bouncing in her throat. "Phil is running for re-election. Leigh Anne Saddler is the ex-model trying to ruin him."

"What business did a former model and a senator-elect have in common? How did they meet?"

Mia heard the doubt in his voice and forced back a scream. "It's not what you think. My brother is telling the truth. Leigh Anne Saddler works at one of the big drug companies in Research Triangle Park. They met when Phil was invited to speak at a banquet for Stern-McHamlin employees."

Jake's reaction was all Mia had hoped when she named one of the state's largest employers. Stern-McHamlin Pharmaceuticals produced drugs for a worldwide market. She couldn't turn on the TV to watch any program without seeing several of their commercials. Holding her breath, she waited for him to speak.

Muscles bunched along the square line of his jaw. For a second, she thought he turned pale, but his voice seemed normal when he finally spoke. "What evidence does this model have?"

"That's just it, I don't know. But she claims to have proof Phil tried to pay her off." Mia met his probing stare as she repeated the ex-model's words.

"What does that have to do with the courthouse? She couldn't hide files in there without being seen."

"The judge ordered her to turn over all evidence, but Friday, Leigh Anne claimed she'd misplaced some files."

"You don't believe her?"

Mia returned his stare. "Leigh Anne was quoted, saying she has evidence to prove her claims against Phil."

"What does that have to do with you sneaking past security to get into the courthouse?"

Mia's cheeks warmed. "I think Leigh Anne hid a disc in the courtroom to keep from turning files over to the judge."

"Why the courtroom? Why not a place she has easy access to in case she needs to retrieve the information?"

Mia blinked at the cold reason in his tone. For half a second she stared at the muscles in the arm he rested on the table. She jerked her gaze away and forced her mind away from how appealing he looked in a t-shirt and back to convincing him to believe her.

"I think she had the disc at the hearing, but when the judge ordered her to turn all files over to the court she changed her mind and hid the disc. If the judge ordered a search of her home, she wouldn't have the evidence and being held in contempt of court."

"Twisted, but believable," Jake studied her across the table. "How did you come up with this angle?"

"It's the only solution I could imagine." Mia stiffened at the doubt in his tone. "The judge ordered her to turn all copies of her files over to the court. None were found in her house or safety deposit box. Where else could they be?"

"I can think of a dozen places."

Lifting her chin high, Mia glared. "Name one."

"Friends. Co-workers. Attorney."

Drumming her fingernails on the table as his sensible response filled the silence, she mumbled. "I said one."

"Just making a point—"

"You don't believe me, do you?"

"If you were a judge, would you believe this story?"

Mia jumped out of the chair. "Can we go now? I have to work tomorrow," she glanced at the clock over the counter, "I mean today."

Jake pushed his chair back and stood.

Her breath caught and she grabbed the back of the chair to keep from falling. He was taller and bigger than she had realized. A head taller than she was, and all muscle. The turnout gear had hidden his strength.

Jake dropped some bills on the table and motioned her toward the door. "I should take you to the police station."

Mia stepped out the door to the sidewalk and looked back over her shoulder. "How will you explain your actions over the last few hours—"

Jake let out a howl of outrage.

Thinking she had him cornered, Mia looked over her shoulder with a gloating grin, but the instant she saw his face in the dim light from the restaurant, she froze. Jake was staring at his truck with astonishment and rage lining his face. Mia followed the direction of his glance and her mouth dropped open.

The tires on his truck had been slashed.

"Son of a gun," Jake snarled as he examined a front tire. "Who the hell did this?"

Her heart slamming against her ribs, Mia tore her eyes from the tires and searched the shadows of the parking lot. "Do you believe me now?"

Jake glared over his shoulder. "Are you suggesting this is connected to the story you just told me?"

She didn't need her skills as a reporter to realize he hadn't believed a word she had said. *Great. Just great.* She had an arsonist trying to kill her and a tire-slasher following them, but this firefighter didn't believe her.

"Have you ever heard of anyone in this town having four slashed tires at the same time, before now?" Clenching her arms around her middle, she tapped the toe of a black shoe on the pavement.

Hands on his hips, Jake walked around the truck. Disbelief marred his face. "Guess I'll call the police after all."

Following close on his heels, Mia gasped. "You can't. Please, Jake. No police."

"What's wrong with calling the police? I didn't say I would turn you in."

"Police reports are listed in the paper. If my name appears in print, I'm in trouble."

"With your brother? Why wouldn't he appreciate your efforts to help?"

"My boss will make my life a living hell if my name appears in the news."

Jake rolled his eyes and stared at the tires. Finally, he walked back to the restaurant and stuck his head in the door. "Hey, Doris, I've got a flat. Can I borrow your car?"

�🚲

Ten minutes later, Jake turned the borrowed Corolla toward Raleigh. At this late hour, Hwy 64 was nearly deserted. "Give me directions to your apartment."

Mia tried every angle she could think of to avoid telling him where she lived. Finally, after all her excuses failed, she gave him her address. "How am I supposed to get my car?"

"It's probably blocked in. You couldn't get it tonight anyway."

"That's it? You're holding my car hostage?"

Cutting a glance toward her, he grinned. "No law against that. Now, holding you until I get answers could cause trouble."

"This isn't a joking matter. I'm serious about finding evidence to clear my brother." Mia twisted in the passenger seat to get a better view of his face in the dim lights from the dash. "I have to get back inside the courthouse and find Leigh Anne's proof. After what you said about files, I'm convinced she stored the information on a thumb drive."

"You know that sounds insane, right? What are the chances of finding a plastic disc after that fire?" Jake's brows arched.

"I know it sounds crazy." Mia shrugged, searching for words to assure him of her sanity. "But I have to work with what clues I've got. Isn't that part of your job? You go with the evidence? I think Leigh Anne hid a disc drive in that courtroom during the hearing. Finding those files is the only way I can prove my brother is innocent."

"What makes you so certain he is?"

Could he read her mind? Had her eyes twitched or her ears wiggled? What could she say?

"He's my brother. I love him. He won election by public opinion, you know." She glared at Jake as if he had said she had an ugly baby. "Phil loves his wife and kids. He's honest and can't be bought. Leigh Anne Saddler works for a drug company worth big bucks--"

"Whoa," Jake stared through the dim light from the dash, "what does the drug company have to do with this complaint against your brother? Other than that's how he met the model?"

"Phil is campaigning against big business, pharmaceutical companies, specifically. He wants to help lower the cost of prescription drugs. I think Leigh Anne's company tried to buy him off and he refused."

Air hissed through his teeth as Jake shook his head. "I should have known."

"What?" Mia's word ended in a squeal as Jake sent the vehicle into a sliding U-turn. At least, she hoped he was in control of the lurching vehicle. "Where did you learn to drive, watching reruns of the Rockford Files on TV?"

There was that word, again. *Files.* Heart racing, she gripped the edge of the seat, and held on tight. Jake drove the car, bumping and bucking across the median, and her head banged against the roof of the car. "Ouch."

He cursed under his breath as the car jumped over the grassy strip between the four-lane highway. "Try to do one good deed—"

Mia's head banged the roof again. "Owww, Will you slow down? We'll get a ticket."

Pushing the gas pedal to the floor, Jake sent the small car rocketing back toward town. He did not understand the blind devotion and faith Mia had in her brother. Growing up in foster homes, he couldn't imagine that kind of trust. The closest he had ever come to having a real family had been his short marriage to Sara.

And look how that turned out.

He had put his firefighter training before Sara's wishes and betrayed her. She wanted them to have a family weekend. He wanted to attend a weekend of training session. If he had shown his wife the unquestioning devotion Mia had for her brother, a drunk driver might not have had a chance to kill his wife and son.

Since the fateful night when he lost everything he loved, he had lived to protect and assert justice for all. By focusing his efforts, he worked to save others. Staring at the road illuminated by the car's headlights, he realized he admired Mia's belief in family. A family of his own was the one thing he had always longed for.

After events with Sara and his son, he experienced firsthand the pain of loss. That explained his strong reaction to Mia. He wanted to spare her the pain he had experienced. He hadn't listened to his wife, but her death had taught him a hard lesson. He listened to Mia. Heard every word she said, even the ones she left unspoken. He couldn't turn away and leave her in danger.

Now that someone had gone to the trouble to slash his tires, he suspected there was more involved with Mia's search than hidden files about a terminated pregnancy.

When she mentioned the drug company, she confirmed his suspicion.

Chapter Four

Moments after the car stopped bucking and swaying, Mia peeped out of one eye and saw they were on asphalt, headed back toward town. Did Jake believe her? Warm fuzzes fluttered in her stomach as she considered the possibility. And just that fast, her situation got worse. Having Jake believe her meant she couldn't keep secrets from him. "Will you slow down?"

"Tell me the truth."

"Why don't you believe me?"

"You're saying you put your life at risk to save your brother's political career. Who would do that? It doesn't make sense."

"How could I know someone would set fire to the courthouse while I was inside?"

Jake shook his head. "You mentioned your boss's reaction if he spotted your name in the paper. If you'd been arrested, your name would appear in the paper."

"I didn't plan on getting caught."

"Like I said, makes no sense."

Darkness closed in on her. Regret and a rush of other emotions reached out of the black night, adding to the ache in her heart, and to the loneliness surrounding her since her father died.

"It does if you played the cow's tail all your life." Lips clamped tight, she clutched her arms across her chest and stared straight ahead. *Why had she said that?*

Dropping speed below ninety, Jake glanced in her direction.

"Cow's tail? What does that mean? You grew up on a farm?"

"Could you slow down? Deer cause frequent accidents on this road, you know."

Jake eased back to eighty. "Talk to me."

Mia expelled a sigh. She had brought this on herself, but why now. Why reveal her darkest emotions to this man. In the short time since they met, she had learned enough about Jake to admire him. But her last words had ruined her chance of improving his impression of her. Why had she spewed off about her issues with sibling rivalry, making her look silly?

Mulling over options as dark shadows along the road flashed by, she finally decided the truth was all that would work and heaved a sign. Once she started revealing details, where would it end? What did she know about Jake? Had he come from a loving family, the whole Walton scenario, or would his instincts as a judge dig deeper? Would he question her lack of details? Or suspect her of hiding the truth.

The truth.

How did anyone know what was true? The word truth had such an honorable sound, and held the promise of justice...but what did it really mean? Uncovering the truth about Phil's private life just skimmed the surface. What about the true reason she was determined to uncover the model's evidence? Her motives weren't honorable or just, but something darker...uglier.

"I doubt my mother would survive if anything happened to my brother."

"She would still have you."

"You think that matters?" Mia turned away, wishing she had kept her mouth shut. "It's not the same."

"Why is that?" Jake stole a glance at her rigid profile. He didn't have a long history with family dynamics. His experience at being part of a real family had ended after four short years of marriage. For those four years, he had basked in feelings of loving and being loved in return. Didn't parents love all of their children, equally? Seeing Mia's stiff-armed grip on the car's dash and wide eyes, he eased back on the gas some more. "You don't think your mother loves you."

It wasn't a question, and the baldly stated words ate at Mia's brain like drops of acid. She shivered. "It...that's not...Phil is special, that's all."

"Because he's a politician?"

Mia closed her eyes and forced words past clenched teeth. "Because he's her son."

Jake eased the speed back to sixty-five. Curiosity built as he studied Mia's silhouette. Any person in their right mind would think Mia Clark was special. Little girls were special. Their mothers dressed them in frills and dads spoiled them. What was wrong with Mia's mother? All children were special.

"Don't miss the exit."

Jake rolled his eyes, not liking his distraction or the memories of his own child taking control of his head. "When we get to the courthouse, we play by my rules. Understand."

"If you think I'm staying in the car, while you go look around, you're wrong."

"Lock the doors if you don't feel safe sitting in the dark."

Mia tore her gaze from the road whizzing past in their headlights and turned a drop-dead glare on him. Not that he bothered to look at her. "I'm going with you."

"You're not authorized—"

"That maniac slashed your tires. I'm not waiting around for my throat to be his next target."

Jake kept his eyes glued to the road. The words, slashed your tires, echoed in his head as did her determined voice. "Don't make a move unless I say you can."

Mia flashed him a grin. "You're the boss. Don't forget, that waitress called you a hero."

Jake muttered a string of words under his breath. This was why life was less complicated when he wasn't involved with a woman. He knew Mia was teasing, but the word hero stabbed at his conscience. If he had been a hero to his wife and child, he wouldn't have lost everything he loved.

Stop. Do not. Go. There. Another woman's life depends on your choices. "The traffic circle will be blocked off. I can get in—"

"Because you're a fireman? Pretend I'm an inspector—"

"It's too dangerous." Jake's firm tone filled the darkness.

"So is waiting in the car for a knife to slit my throat. I need to search for that disc. I'm convinced that's how Leigh Anne hid the information."

Jake glanced in the rearview mirror. A ribbon of light glowed along the eastern skyline. Darkness was their only chance of slipping in undetected. Hell, they probably couldn't get in the building, anyway. "You won't find a disc. Even if it didn't melt, it will look like charred wood and be impossible to detect."

"I have to try." Mia gave him a wide-eyed look. "Your slashed tires prove someone means business. I need that disc to find out why."

⚙

Her first glance of the once graceful old courthouse in the center of town made Mia gasp. The graying dawn light revealed ruins of the building like a gothic painting.

"The roof of the third floor collapsed." The dead tone of Jake's voice sounded as he parked behind a line of official vehicles along the street.

Mia turned to look at him. His words echoed cold with grief in the small car. The mask-like expression on his face made her swallow. Jake looked the way she'd felt when her mother insisted she drop everything and find evidence to clear her brother.

"Do you think they can save—"

"Yeah, but we'll rebuild. The courthouse is part of our history." Jake stepped out of the car and slammed the door, forgetting their mission required stealth.

Mia scrambled out her side and eased the door shut as she nodded toward satellite trucks parked on the other side of the traffic circle."How will we avoid the camera crews?"

"Follow me and stick close." Jake passed his cap to her. "Tuck your hair up. Pull the brim low."

Mia did as he said and stuck close as a shadow as he approached the building. First one firefighter then another called to him.

"Hey, Jake."

"Back to check the damage, Jake?"

"Didn't think you'd stay away long, Jake."

Mia liked the casual tone and respect in the men's voices. Much as she hated to admit it, their deference to the man at her side gave her comfort. After all, she was heading back in the building where someone had tried to kill her, and Jake had been in the building at the same time. For all she knew, Jake could be the arsonist, or the person who shoved her in the closet.

That thought almost made her laugh. Jake loved this stately old building. She had heard the emotion in his voice when he talked about the destruction from the blaze.

The odor of burned wood and smoke filled her nostrils. Every muscle in her body went rigid. Jake had warned her to stay out of the building, but she needed answers. Still, the memory of being trapped and the over-powering stench of smoke almost changed her mind.

Hearing Jake addressed as judge reminded her that he was an officer of the court. A fact she should have considered before she revealed her suspicions to him. Dread washed over her as she stared at the back of his head. What had she done? What if she found the files…and they proved Phil had done something wrong.

Had her efforts to clear her brother's name put him in a more precarious position? Would Jake demand a look at the files if she found them?

Jake turned and noticed she wasn't behind him. Two loping strides brought him back to her side. "Keep up, Clark, if you want to get inside before cameras catch you on film."

"Don't use my name. Reporters might hear," she hissed. When this was over, she intended to get some answers from Jake Stone. Like, why he cared so much about the courthouse, and why he was so rigid. She couldn't ask now. The acrid stench from the fire stole her breath away.

The terror of the previous night's events rushed back, slapping her in the face. Her stomach sloshed. The stench of ashes burned her memory, but her mother's demands forced her to put one foot in front of the other and follow Jake.

Once they were inside the door, Jake made a quick inspection of the ceiling and walls on the first floor, and motioned Mia forward. "Where to?"

Knees wobbly, Mia moved close to his side. "Is it safe?"

Jake gave her a long searching stare. "Being inside a burned building is never safe, but the damage here is mostly from water. Have you changed your mind?"

Not wanting to admit the nausea churning in her stomach, Mia shook her head. "Can we get to the records room?"

"Watch your footing." Jake picked his way through two doors

and slowly inched up the stairs. Some steps were littered with ceiling tiles that had fallen after getting soaked. Stopping in a doorway of the records room, he surveyed the damage, and sent her a look over his shoulder. "I don't think you're going to have any luck finding a disc in this room."

There was more damage in this room than in the hallway. Tiles from the ceiling formed a soggy heap on top of water-spattered papers littering the floor.

Overturned file cabinets explained the mass of paper. Water had washed soot and partially burned objects through the gaps left when the ceiling tiles fell.

Glancing around at knee-deep piles of debris, Mia agreed. Finding evidence in this mess would take a miracle. Breathing through her mouth, to keep out the odor, she studied the destruction and nearly admitted defeat. But she couldn't quit, now. Someone had almost killed her in an effort to keep her from finding the truth. "I almost died in this room, I can't give up. I need to check the courtroom."

"Are you sure?"

Mia turned away, not daring to meet his eye and let him see her fear. "There's still a chance the files are hidden in there."

She felt Jake's eyes bore into her back, but after long seconds, he moved past her and picked a path across the hall. "Watch your step."

"Will the floor hold us?" Mia froze in place.

"The fire was on the roof. This floor should be safe."

"Judge Stone?" A man's voice called from the direction of the stairs.

Jake turned toward the sound. "Yes?"

"It's not safe for you to be in here. The fire inspector hasn't arrived yet."

Mia stood behind Jake, afraid to move. She was so close to finding answers, please don't stop us now. She had overcome her fear of returning to the room where she'd been trapped and breathed in the stench of burned wood. She couldn't stop now.

"I'll be careful, Tim. Let me know when the inspector gets here. I want to hear what he thinks started this fire."

"Me, too, Judge. Just be careful."

As the man's voice faded away, Mia let go the breath she'd

been holding. "I didn't search the courtroom yesterday. I might have missed something."

Jake looked up from the rubble on the floor and frowned at her. "How long were you in the building?"

Mia shrugged, lowering her eyes to find a place to take her next step. "Thirty minutes, maybe."

Remembering he was an officer of the court and could reprimand the security staff, she clamped her lips shut. She didn't want to get anyone in trouble because she was over zealous about clearing her brother.

"I want to catch the bastard who did this," Jake snarled, staring around the ruined courtroom.

Black sludge and dripping water coated everything. The acrid odor of smoke and wet soot filled the air, making it hard to breathe. Nothing in the room had burned, but water and smoke stain covered everything.

Hearing the pain and anger in Jake's voice and seeing the damage, Mia's shoulders slumped. She wanted the arsonist caught, too. And for more reasons than her suspicion that it was the same person who attacked her. "Where would you hide something in this room?"

"I wouldn't. And neither would you."

Mia arched a brow, studying Jake's scowling expression. "Why not?"

"This courtroom is not open to the public. If your girl hid anything in this room, it was while court was in session."

Mia opened her mouth, but snapped her lips shut when a scrapping noise echoed loud in the early morning air. Heart hammering in her throat, she turned a startled glance on Jake.

He motioned her to keep quiet, but the sound wasn't repeated.

Pulse racing, Mia shivered. Was the person who slashed the truck tires in the building, waiting for them, ready to slash more than tires this time?

"Okay, Judge," she snapped, "where would you hide a small object in this room?"

Jake paused in middle of the courtroom, and looked around. Wooden benches lay in disarray, some overturned on the floor. "Here"

If Mia hadn't been with Jake for hours, his deadly tone would have scared the life out of her, but one look at his rigid jaw and the fists clenched at his sides, showed his reaction to seeing his court-room in shambles.

But she fought back the urge to offer a comforting hug. Keeping her distance from Jake was the only way she could protect her tumbling emotions. "Where?"

"Look under tables and benches. Don't move anything."

Mia opened her mouth to ask him exactly how was she suppos-ed to do that, but Jake had started searching the bottom of tables nearest him.

She moved to the opposite side of the room and began looking. Her eyes watered. Her nose burned. The churning in her stomach threatened to return those pancakes any second. But she remember-ed her mother's distress about the former model's words in the pa-per, and forced her mind to concentrate on deep breathing.

Deep breaths added to her nausea, but she kept searching. The need to clear her brother's name and prove she bore him no ill will kept her moving when her eyes started running, making it hard to see.

After inspecting the bottom of numerous benches and the many blobs of gun stuck there, Mia's hopes dwindled. There were only five benches left to check on her side of the room. Five chances to find Leigh Anne Saddler's evidence.

Knees shaking from fear of failure, not just failing to clear her brother, but not finding evidence to clear her family's name, she checked under the next long wooden bench. Amid the dark stains and gum wads, she spotted a larger blob. Something purple, like so many of the wads of gum, but this mound didn't look like gum.

Even in the dim morning light, the glint of purple against the dark wood started her heart pounding. Gum did not reflect light. "Jake. Look."

Jake stopped his search and moved her side. Before he could speak, the sound of loud footsteps crunched in the hall outside the room. Jake made a quick motion with his hand for Mia to be quiet and turned toward the door.

Instinct caused Mia to glance around the room for a place to hide, but she forced her feet to stay put. It could be firefighters, or the inspector, but why hadn't they heard voices? Almost having the evidence in her hand and have someone take it away from her was unthinkable.

But even worse was the stealthy sound of movement so near them. Because they were just looking, and not moving the benches, they had made little noise. Did the person outside the door know they were here? Had someone followed them, or had the arsonist returned to the scene of the crime?

Was the slasher and the person who shoved her in the closet the same person? Or were they dealing with three threats? Would the slasher take the risk of other firefighters seeing him and follow them into the building?

With questions whirling in her head, she paused for about two seconds and watched Jake ease toward the door. Then, fueled by fear of the unknown, she tried to pry the thumb disc loose from the bench. But the small object was stuck hard to the wood. The shape was deformed, but it was definitely a thumb disc.

Biting her lip, she tried to force the disc loose. Whatever Leigh Anne had used to stick the plastic to the bottom of the bench had worked. Mia pulled and tugged, but eased pressure when she couldn't budge the plastic loose.

"You found it?"

Mia jumped a foot. Heart pounding she faced Jake and felt warmth rush to her cheeks. He couldn't read her mind. Could he guess she planned to hide the disc in her pocket while the intruder distracted him? Oh, well... "It's stuck."

Angling his body so he could keep one eye on the door, Jake leaned over to examine the bottom of the bench.

Mia studied the tense expression on his face. "Do you think someone followed us?"

"Nope, the fire inspector probably arrived early."

"You told that fireman to call you—"

"This building is a crime scene until all the evidence is in. People forget in the excitement."

"A-are we tampering with evidence?" Mia swallowed fears of being arrested and having her name in news. She would definitely lose her job. Probably ruin Phil's chances at re-election, and earn her mother's displeasure, as well.

"I know what to look for at a crime scene." Jake held her gaze for long seconds, then turned back to the bench. "If I find any evidence pointing to arson, the inspector will be the first one to know."

Did that mean he wouldn't give her the disc? As much as she admired his determination, part of her wanted to choke him, but one glance at his broad chest ended that thought. She wanted to get her hands on Jake, all right, but not to choke him...unless it was with her arms wrapped tightly around his neck. Oh, help! "Can you twist it off?"

"What did she use to stick this thing on?"

"Nail polish?" Mia pointed to the red blotch on the edge of the disc.

"In my courtroom?"

Forcing back a smile at the note of outrage in his tone, Mia shrugged. "Leigh Anne is a former model. Nail polish is something she would carry in her handbag. Nothing else makes sense."

Jake gave a twist and straightened, holding the disc between two fingers. "I wonder what's on this—"

A loud screeching noise sounded close and echoed loudly in the early morning quiet. Mia hadn't noticed the absence of traffic noise until she heard loud steps pounding on the wood floor, followed and the sound of a door opening.

Fear exploded inside her and blocked her throat. She couldn't breathe. The walls of the room swayed and wrinkled. Spots danced in front of her eyes. Memory of being trapped in that dark closet flooded her head. Knees wobbling, she realized she was in danger of making a fool of herself and falling at Jake's feet.

Jake.

She couldn't pass out in front of Jake. Not after he helped her get inside the building. Bracing her hands on her knees, bending her head down, she focused on taking deep breaths as she pretended to check on the overturned bench at her feet.

After a few seconds, her head cleared, but another loud noise filled the air. She jerked upright and eyes wide, she glanced at Jake. "What was that?"

Jake shoved the disc in his pocket and grabbing her arm, he turned to the door. His fingers brushed against her side, sending a jolt of awareness through her body. Her muddled senses jerked to alert as the felt the heat of his touch, but she forced her attention on the danger around them. This was not the time to react to Jake's touch.

"I don't know, but it was human." Jake pulled her behind him, using his body to shield her as he edged toward the door. "Stay close and watch your step. We need to check the records room."

Mia clamped her lips shut and tried to ignore the heat raging through her limbs. Jake had barely touched her, but her nerves burned with awareness. And responding to Jake was the last thing she needed.

Her reaction was just one more reference to fire, heat, burning…all the things that caused her to lose control of her life. First her mother's insistence that she risk danger to save her brother, and now an officer of the court, who could turn her in to police at any second, fired her senses to full alert.

Worse, Jake didn't believe she was telling him the truth. Even with heat flaring between them when their bodies touched, she could see doubt burning in his eyes. What had she gotten herself into?

She stopped moving. Her feet stuck firmly to the floor as memories took hold of her. "We already checked in there."

"That's were the noise came from," Jake glanced over his shoulder, "come on, Clark. I can't leave you here by yourself."

Teeth gritted, Mia followed so close when he stopped in the hall, she almost collided against his back. Jake glanced over his shoulder and put a finger against his lips, then cocked his head to the side, listening.

Then she heard the sound of footsteps pounding down the stairs filled the early morning quiet. Jake let go her hand and turned to give chase. Mia grabbed his arm. "Do you think it's the slasher? What was he doing here?"

"Back to finish the job," Jake tried to shake her hand off, "let go. I need to go after him."

"No, you can't. Remember your tires?"

"Are you trying to protect me?" Jake asked over his shoulder as he pulled her through the burned rubble on the floor. "I thought you couldn't wait to get rid of me."

"If you end up dead, police will think I did it." Mia tried to keep her voice calm. Begging him to stay was the last thing she wanted, but how could she get out of the building, or avoid arrest, without him? She motioned to the door across the all. "You wanted to check in here."

A grinding screech filled the air. Jake's body stiffened. He turned a hard stare on her. "Too late, he's already gone. That grinding noise came from the backdoor."

Jake rushed inside the records room and scrambled over piles of debris littering the floor so he could look out the window on the far wall. "He's wearing black and his head's covered with a hood."

Mia heard the implication in his words and glanced down at her black attire. Was the way she was dressed the reason Jake didn't believe her?

"What was he doing here?" She stared at the piles of ceiling tiles littering the room as tension gripped her body. That Jake didn't show any response when they touched was bad, but knowing he blamed her for the damaged courthouse was worse. "How did he get in? Where was he hiding that we didn't see him?"

Jake picked a path around the littered floor, stepping carefully around charred debris. In one corner of the room, the pile of blackened trash stood taller that the rest. Chills chased along Mia's spine as she followed his gaze to that corner of the room.

"I don't remember seeing a pile this big." Jake approached the mound of rubble.

Noticing his tense posture, Mia followed his steps, slowly picking her way through the debris. "Do you see anyth—"

"What the," frowning, Jake lifted a ceiling tile with the toe of his boot and leaned over to look under the tile, "stay back."

About the time he spoke, Mia spotted the soot covered blonde hair he had exposed and let out a gasp. Was a woman caught in the fire? Thoughts of her own narrow escape made her stomach slosh at the thought. "Is she—"

"Dead." Jake stared at Mia with dark troubled eyes. "This room was clear before the fire got bad. I searched it myself."

The guilt in his tone wrenched at Mia's heart. In the short time she had been with Jake, she had learned how much he cared about people. Look at the way he had rescued her. Biting her lip to steady her nerves, she eased closer. "Does she work here? Do you recognize her?"

Jake's brow lifted, his glance turned cold. A cold, accusing expression covered his face as he stared at her. "Don't you?"

What had brought suspicion back to his voice? Jake hadn't believed her reason for being in the courthouse, but surely, he didn't think she was capable of hurting someone. Clenching her fists, Mia looked closer at the blonde hair and gasped as the reason for Jake's sudden renewal of suspicion hit her. "Is it—"

"The model," Jake said as his stare sharp as an ice pick. "If I hadn't checked this room two minutes before I found you crumpled in the hall, I would think you had something to do with this."

"Me?" Mia straightened upright, wounded more by his words than she wanted to admit. When had Jake's good opinion of her started to matter? "We were in this room ten minutes ago." She moved to take a closer look. Only one woman would make Jake accuse her of murder. "You're sure it's the—"

"Leigh Anne Saddler? I think so, from the looks of that blonde hair and her uh...obviously enhanced physical attributes."

Mia turned wide eyes on Jake. "I didn't do this. You have to believe me. I could never intentionally hurt someone, no more than I would set fire to this building."

"But we haven't proved you didn't set that fire, now have we, Ms. Clark?"

His accusations slashed her skin causing pain she couldn't describe. Hadn't he learned a thing about her in the hours they had spent together? Did he really believe she could commit a criminal act? What kind of judge was he, if he was that far off reading of her character? "You don't really think…"

Her words trailed off. Emotion clogged her throat. None of this made sense, but since Jake had saved her life, she cared about his opinion. She wanted him to believe in her. Trust her. With his position, if she made one wrong step, Jake could ruin her career and her brother's. But there was more at stake here than her career.

Jake had saved her life. She wanted him to think she was worth the risk he had taken with his own safety. Clearing her throat, she tried again. "You don't think I killed Leigh Anne, do you?"

Jake looked in her eyes for long seconds, and shook his head. "No. The question is. Who did?" He stared at the body without touching anything. "Her throat was cut."

"Slit?" Mia grabbed her throat, forcing back the horror building inside her. She gulped deep breaths until her lungs burned from the stench of smoke and her eyes watered. How close had the murderer been? Close enough to use a knife blade? "The tire slasher?"

"Maybe," Jake motioned toward the pile of rubble. "Someone

left her body here to make it look like she died in the fire."

"Who would do this? Was it a man? Could you tell?"

"Best guess? I'd say it had to be a man to get the body up those stairs." Jake's gaze bored into her. "Since I found you in the building," he paused, "that leaves you and your brother as the prime suspects."

"But...you just said you searched this room right before you found me."

"Yeah," his eyes bored into her as if trying to read her mind.

Mia felt as if he touched her very core, where the pain of his words centered, deep in her heart. Hadn't he learned a thing about her since they met? How could he think she could do this terrible thing? "But—"

"That leaves your brother—"

"Hey, Jake," a man called, "are you up there? The fire inspector is here. He called a meeting on the front steps."

"I'm coming, Tim." Jake stared at Mia for long seconds as noise of the firefighter's steps disappeared. "Considering the circumstances, I can't believe what I'm about to do." Eyes dark with emotion, he studied her. "For the second time in twenty-four hours I'm helping you slip out of this courthouse undetected."

A sigh quivered past Mia's lips. "You believe me?"

Jake's jaw clenched. "I'm reserving judgment."

Chapter Five

Mia shoved her fists in her jean pockets to keep from pounding that superior look off Jake's face. Her fingers touched metal. Her car keys. "I don't need your help this time. Give me the disc and I'll leave. Then you won't have to feel guilty about helping me."

Jake held up the disc. "Is this all you care about?"

Mia gave a nod, but his gaze sliced her conscience. "No, but I'll take care of other things after I've cleared my brother."

"Judge Stone? Are you coming?" Tim's voice bounced off the walls, mingling with the sounds of early morning traffic.

"Coming," Jake called as he took a step toward Mia. "Aren't you forgetting something?"

Shaking her head, Mia held her hand out. "The disc is all the evidence I need."

Jake nodded toward the mound of debris in the corner. "What about the body?"

Eyes squeezed shut, Mia sighed. "I'm sorry Leigh Anne is dead, but I didn't have anything to do with her death. I need to get to a computer and open that disc."

"You're forgetting a few facts." Jake dangled the disc in his fingers. "You had a motive, the means, and the opportunity."

"I didn't even know she was in the building." Mia kept her voice low, forcing words past gritted teeth to keep her lips from quivering. Voices carried in empty buildings. "I couldn't kill anyone, even Leigh Anne. All I wanted was the evidence."

Brow arched, he reached in his pocket and pulled out his cell phone. "You're defending your family's honor. That's a strong motive for murder."

"What are you doing?" Mia gasped as he punched numbers on the phone. "I didn't—"

"Sh—" Jake held up a finger. "Chief, this is Jake Stone. Yeah, how are you Bob? Yeah, me too. Listen, Chief, I'm over at the courthouse. Yes, I know the fire marshals called a meeting. They're here now, but I need your help on the second floor of the courthouse—"

Wincing, Jake held the phone away from his ear.

"Yeah. I know, but this is my courthouse. I wanted to see the damage. Listen, I called because while I was looking around, I stumbled over a body. No. I didn't move anything. Get over here quick. I caught a glimpse of someone sneaking away from the building. I'm going to follow him. I'll call you if I see him, again."

Jake shoved the phone in his pocket and stared at Mia. "We have about five minutes to get out of here."

"You don't have to do this," Mia found herself offering as she stepped closer. "Helping me means breaking every oath of your office. Give me the disc and go meet with the inspectors."

"Don't you get it?" Jake edged toward the door. "Both of us were in this building. We could be the intended victims. It might be our fault that woman is dead." He snapped his lips shut and headed toward the stairs, "We both have a connection to the victim."

Mia eased down the stairs behind him. "You didn't even know Leigh Anne Saddler."

"She appeared in my courtroom and made a mockery of the justice system I've sworn to uphold."

"Oh, come on, Judge. That motivation is so slim it's almost invisible," Mia whispered, following close on his heels as he led the way toward the back exit. "Listen to me, Jake. You don't have to risk your career to help me. Give me the disc. I'll send you copies of anything I find."

Jake grabbed her elbow and urged her toward the door. "Show me how you escaped last night without anyone seeing you."

"Are you sure? I can take my car and be gone in—"

"Go. We don't have time to argue." Jake glanced around the lawn surrounding the courthouse and urged her out.

Bending down, Mia took the lead, darting from one shrub to the next. When they reached the corner of the building, she nodded to the street opposite. "I crossed here."

Crouching low, Jake followed her across the street. Once they reached the sidewalk, he turned in the opposite direction. "I left the car over here—"

He stopped mid-step, his words still hanging in the damp morning air.

Mia plowed into him from behind. "What—"

After following his glance, she didn't need an explanation. Even in the early morning light, she could see the tires of their borrowed car had been slashed. Chills raced through her body. Teeth chattering, she asked, "W-who—"

"This answers one question." Jake searched the street in both directions. "Obviously, we were the killer's targets." He grabbed her elbow as his gaze swept the area. Evidently seeing nothing, he turned in the opposite direction, keeping Mia at his side. "Let's get going. We'll take your car."

So we don't end up like Leigh Anne Saddler.

He didn't say the words aloud, but Mia heard them in the tone of his voice and moved closer to his side. "I don't remember where I parked."

Jake clamped her arm against his body and headed toward the corner where she remembered talking to the waitress yesterday. "I can guess. We can't stay here."

Mia skipped to keep up with his long stride as he crossed the street. Thankful no cars were passing and they didn't have to stand exposed on the corner, she darted a look over her shoulder as they left the shelter of the buildings along the sidewalk.

"This means the killer followed us, doesn't it? He knows we were searching the building. Do you think he knows what we were looking for?"

Jake urged her past the street she had searched yesterday before he caught up with her and headed on around the traffic circle to the next street. "If he didn't, once he spotted Leigh Anne Saddler, he worked it out."

"But why kill her?" Mia glanced over her shoulder, again.

"Don't do that." Jake pulled her against his side. "Checking behind you makes you look guilty. Just walk normal and no one will pay any attention."

"Are you kidding?" Mia gave a snort of disbelief and sent him a sideways glance. Any woman with breath left in her body would notice Jake Stone from a mile away. "We don't look like early morning joggers."

"You'd be surprised."

Those words were barely out of his mouth, when a woman in her mid-fifties stepped off her lawn onto the sidewalk to pick up her newspaper. "Out early aren't you, Judge?"

"Late night," Jake replied without slowing his step.

"It's such a shame about the courthouse, but walking is smart. Get that smoke out of your lungs and you'll feel better." The woman kept talking as they passed.

"See," Jake cut a glance at Mia. "She didn't notice a thing. Now, where is your car?"

Mia spotted her Honda Accord parked along the street, three cars up. Pulling the keys out of her pocket, she said, "There it is. I'll driv—"

"Do you have control issues, Ms. Clark, or is this a reflection on my driving?"

Mia gave a snort and jerked the door open. "Where are we going? The slasher attacked your truck, so he must know you."

"Good point," Jake settled in the passenger seat and buckled his seatbelt, "but if he's smart enough to work out what we were looking for, he's figured out who you are by now. Take the next right." He drummed his fingers on the dash as she headed toward Hwy 64. "That means we can't go to your place or mine."

Mia groaned. "I need a shower. I'm filthy."

"You're alive," Jake stared across the small space separating them. "Now tell me. What's really going on, Ms. Clark?"

"I told you, Leigh Anne—"

"Is dead. If you don't want to end up the same way, tell me what's going on."

Mia trembled as his words hammered the truth into her head. Dead. The vibrant ex-model she had wanted to hate when she saw her in court three days ago was dead. And the person who killed her could have been the same person who...

"Do you think the killer is the person who locked me in that closet?"

"If it is, I'd say you are lucky. Tell me the truth—"

"I have." Mia pushed down the gas pedal. "You know everything I know. The missing information must be on that disc."

"I don't think so. Do you know where you're going?"

"No." That one word blared repeatedly in her head. The things she didn't know could get them both killed.

↻

Jake's cell phone rang.

"Keep heading east," he said, lifting the phone to his ear. "Stone, here."

Mia gripped the wheel and tried to keep her eyes on the road. It wasn't easy. Her gaze darted to the rear-review mirror every two seconds. What was she expecting to see? Some car flying a flag that said, I'm following you.

Jake's caution about avoiding their homes added to her worry. So did the tension she heard in his voice.

"Chief, I can't come right now. I'm following the person I saw leave the building. Did you find the body? Was there any identification?" Staring straight ahead, Jake sighed. "Yeah, I remember the name from the newspapers. Leigh Anne Saddler appeared in court last Friday."

Shivers chased down Mia's spine. She had known the body must be the ex-model, but having the identity confirmed made things worse.

A person with connection to Phil was murdered. What had her brother gotten into? Was he in danger? Worse, did Phil have anything to do with this murder? The sound of Jake's voice close at her side added to her panic. He would suspect Phil, first and ask questions later.

"I know, Chief. I just wanted to check the damage in my courtroom. I heard a noise across the hall. With the building supposedly empty—"

Wincing, Jake hunched his shoulders. "Yeah, I know that meant me, too, but that courtroom is my life. I was careful—"

He held the phone away from his ear and exchanged glances with Mia. "I can't come to the station right now. I think the person who killed that model was after me."

Mia heard a loud screech from the phone.

"Why? Eight reasons, that's why. Someone slashed the tires on my truck last night. I borrowed a car to get back to the courthouse this morning. When I ran out to follow the guy I saw, the tires of my borrowed car had been slashed."

Mia watched muscles bulge along Jake's jaw. He was stalling, but what if he was wrong? Shivers raced over her. What if she was the target, not Jake?

He hadn't mentioned her name to the chief. She appreciated that, but what if this whole thing had something to do with her investigation for Phil. Police would be on the wrong track.

Jake had left the scene of a crime to help her. That meant he was risking his career to keep her safe. She couldn't let him take that chance. Making a split second decision, she whipped the steering wheel and turned off on the approaching exit.

Brows arched, Jake held her gaze. "I realize that, Chief, but I can take care of myself. If you don't have to assign men to protect me, you can put more men in the search for the killer."

Mia tensed, preparing to face his objections as she turned into the parking lot of a large gas station. She wanted a bath and food. And sleep. Then maybe her brain could make sense of what was going on.

Jake snapped the phone shut. "I thought we were going to Raleigh."

Mia turned the engine off and twisted in the seat to face him. "Why? The problem is here."

"We're going to Raleigh because there is a killer on our trail."

"We don't know who the killer is. We don't even know if it's a man or a woman. We're covered in soot, and starved." Mia tilted her chin. "I need a shower and clean clothes."

And a chance to see what's on that disc.

Frowning, Jake glanced around the parking lot. "You're right."

Mia's eyes widened. "I am?"

"We need funds."

"I locked my handbag in the trunk. I'll get my credit card." She reached for the door, but Jake put his hand on her arm.

"No, we need cash. Once the local police report the murder to the SBI, they might start looking for us. First thing they will do is put a trace our credit cards." Jake stared down at the cell phone and frowned. "And our phones."

"Now you're scaring me. This isn't a crime show on TV." She shivered, trying to block out images of Leigh Anne Saddler's bloody throat and soot streaked hair, but it was too late. Flashes of the model's marble white face filled her head. Wrapping her arms around her waist to stop the shivers, she looked at Jake. "You are the only one who knows I was there."

"We need a plan. Fill the car with gas. I'll get a map." Jake paused, his hand on the door handle. "On second thought, maybe you should go inside alone. We're still in Courtney County. Someone might recognize me."

Mia fought the urge to glance over her shoulder every two seconds as she filled the Honda with gas. Stepping inside the station, she gave the room a quick search before heading for the cashier. At the last second, with hunger twisting her insides, she added two ice-cold Pepsi bottles and some snacks to her bill.

Returning to the car with her arms full, she paused at the driver's door when she spotted Jake behind the wheel. "Hey."

"Hey, back." Jake nodded toward the passenger seat. "Hop in."

Mia thrust a cold Pepsi in his waiting hand and stomped around the front of the car. Flinging her body in the passenger seat, she slammed the door. "What's going on?"

"I thought I'd drive. I know the area better than you do."

Mia opened her mouth to argue, then noticed him glance in the rear-view mirror and changed her mind. She knew he could drive fast if he needed to. "I'm ready."

"There's a strip mall down the road about a mile. We'll get clean clothes there."

"I need a shower." Looking in the side mirror, Mia checked for cars behind them, but the angle was wrong. She couldn't see if anyone was following them.

Jake turned into the parking lot and stopped at the ATM booth. "We need to get money in case an alert goes out. I don't know how long it will take for the SBI to get curious about us. But we don't need to worry about another tail."

Biting her lip, Mia nodded. Jake knew something and he wasn't telling her. But what? Had the Chief called again? Had Jake told the chief about her part in the morning's events? He and the chief were friends. She could tell that from the conversation she'd overheard earlier. As far as Jake knew, she was an arsonist.

Sighing, she opened the car door. She should have tried to get away from him back at the courthouse when she'd had the chance, even if he did have the disc.

⚙

They decided to play safe and maxed out both their accounts. Then Jake drove across the parking lot and stopped in front of a Dollar General store.

"These stores carry everything." He nodded to the wide double doors. "You'll be safe inside. We shouldn't go in together."

Mia climbed out of the car and turned. Leaning her head in the passenger door, she asked in a low voice. "Should I dye my hair?"

Jake's laugh came from deep in his chest and had a note of enjoyment she hadn't associated with him up to this point. His wide smile and gleaming eyes sent heat racing through her body. What would it be like to spend time with Jake, without this murder hanging over their heads? Fun? Intense? Invigorating?

All that and more, and thinking about the possibilities made her cheeks warm. "People in movies always dye their hair when they're on the run."

"We aren't that desperate, yet." Jake's eyes lost all hint of humor. "We'll take that step later, if we have to."

Mia slammed the door and walked away. Thank goodness, he didn't want her to cut or dye her hair.

Jake watched as Mia entered the store. Checking that no one was following her, he pulled out his phone. They needed a place to stay while they figured out what was going on, and he knew just the person who could help.

It was a risk. Using his phone to call his friend could alert police to their location. A second before he hit the call button, he reconsidered. Images of the model's soot covered body changed his mind. He couldn't put Dan and his family in danger.

He started to put the phone away, paused. Taking the phone apart, he removed the battery, opened the door and smashed the phone under his heel. He hadn't seen much of Dan since the accident, but he couldn't draw attention to the area and risk his friend's safety.

Dan wouldn't mind if Jake used the cabin at the lake. He and Sara had often spent weekends with Dan and his wife, but Jake

56

wanted to make sure the cabin was available.

Mia opened the passenger door and tossed several bags in the back seat. "I bought enough for four days."

Jake cocked his brow. "Did you leave anything in the store?"

"I didn't buy any men's clothing." Mia angled her chin toward the store. "Feel free."

A car pulled in across the parking lot. Jake's humor disappeared. It was too soon to assume they hadn't been followed. Had he been careless by sending Mia in the store alone?

Leaving her in the car seemed even worse. He tapped the steering wheel and checked the rearview mirror. The occupant of the other car went into a store and tension eased from his shoulders. Asking Mia to go back in the store would attract attention. He should have thought this through.

"I don't like leaving you out here alone."

Mia turned wide eyes on him. Was it a trick of light, or had she turned a shade paler under the soot?

"I'll lock the doors."

Jake frowned. "Did the clerk ask questions about the soot on your face?"

"I told her I got close to take pictures of the fire, and now my paper wants me to stay in town for a few days to get more."

"Good thinking." Jake got out. "Lock the doors. If anyone tries to get in, hold down the horn."

Mia watched him cross the sidewalk and enter the store. The emotions filling her chest weren't caused by her uneasy reaction to his words. Even with the coating of soot, Jake was handsome enough to turn heads, hers included. She gasped, realizing the trouble she was in, and new fears exploded in her head.

What should she do? Being with Jake made her heart race, but he didn't trust her. Looking around the parking lot, and not seeing anything suspicious, she pulled out her cell phone. Jake said his calls might be traced, but her phone should be safe since Jake was the only one who knew she'd been in the courthouse. There was no reason for anyone to monitor her calls. She had to take the risk.

⚎

First, she called the newspaper and arranged to take a few days sick leave, then she made the call she dreaded.

"Mother, how are you?" She pressed the phone to her ear to

57

stop her hand shaking.

"Ecstatic, haven't you seen the news? That mudslinging model was found dead."

"Mother!" Mia pressed a hand to her chest and made a quick scan of the parking lot. "She was someone's daughter—"

"She was trying to ruin my son. Don't expect sympathy from me."

The image of Leigh Anne Saddler's body, covered in soot and debris, filled Mia's head. *What if it had been me?* "Mother, I don't have much time. I wanted to check that you're all right."

"Of course, I am. Come over this afternoon for tea."

"Can't, I'm…working…on an interview. Out of town." Mia rolled her eyes and checked the parking lot, again. "If you're all right, I'll let you go."

Jake opened the driver's door.

Mia snapped the phone off.

"Why are you using the phone? I told you we had to be careful." He tossed bags in the back seat and settled behind the wheel.

"I was careful. I needed to check on my mother. And you're the only one who knows I was in that courthouse." Mia watched his strong hands grip the wheel.

Jake gave a grunt. "Right, it should be safe, but from now on," he pulled disposable phones out of a shopping bag, "we use these."

Mia's insides quivered. Trapped in a fire, and finding a body wasn't enough? Now they had to use non-traceable phones.

How had all this happened? How could her mother sound so cold about Leigh Anne's death?

Lost in thought, she didn't speak until Jake assembled the phones and started the car. "Where are we going?"

"Still want food and a bath?"

"You have to ask? Did you find a motel?"

"Better," Jake turned left out of the shopping center and picked up speed. "A friend from law school has a cabin on the lake. We used to come here often."

"We?" Mia arched an inquiring brow.

"My wife and I used to visit Dan and his wife on weekends."

"You're married?"

"She died."

Hearing the abruptness of his tone, and seeing the muscle jerking along his jaw, Mia let the subject drop. Her stomach growled loud enough for him to hear. "Is it far?"

Jake flicked the turn signal and pulled in a fast food parking lot. "I hope not. We need food."

"I'll go in," Mia wiggled out of her seat, "I need the restroom."

"Drop the battery for your cell phone in the commode."

Ten minutes later, with a large bucket of fried chicken scenting up the car, Jake pulled on the road again. "I called Dan. We can use the cabin."

Had he made the right decision?

Mia's life was at risk, and police wanted to question him about the body they discovered in the courthouse.

"How far is it?" Mia stared out the window at nothing but trees. "This road is so secluded it's spooky."

Minutes later, passing mile after mile of pine trees growing in the sandy soil, Jake turned in a narrow drive on the left and slowed the car. Bumping along the trail for another half-mile, he pulled the car to a stop beside a rustic, A-frame, log cabin.

"It's larger on the inside than it looks." Jake nodded toward the house and got out of the car. "It has three bedrooms, two baths and a large great room. We'll be safe here."

"Are you sure your friend won't mind if we use his house? I'd hate to add breaking and entering to my list of offenses."

Chapter Six

After they ate, Mia took a shower, put on the new sweatpants and t-shirt, and returned to the great room. Opening the laptop she retrieved from the trunk of her car, she turned a stern glare on Jake. Firmness and determination were her only weapons against her increasing awareness of Jake. Sharing a car and now, living arrangements, kept them close and personal. She knew what he liked to eat…crust off the chicken first, then the meat, and veggies. Plus, his smoky masculine scent had seared her brain. Remaining bossy and direct was her only hope of keeping in control. "Okay, give me the disc."

Jake dangled the disc out of her reach. "What if the evidence on this disc proves the model's story?" His gaze roamed over her as he asked. "Will you try to erase the disc?"

Mia felt like a science specimen under a microscope as she returned his stare. "I hadn't thought—"

"You're a newspaper reporter. Surely you considered your options." He frowned, tapping the disc on the arm of the chair.

"You're determined to believe the worst about me, aren't you?" Mia tore her gaze from his face and stared at the laptop. Was she afraid of what she would see in his expression? Or worried he could read her mind? Cursing her reaction to a man who could ruin both her career and her brother's with one phone call to chief of police, she held up a staying hand. "Don't answer that question. I don't have a right to question your opinions."

"Are you trying to protect me again, firebird?"

Her head jerked up. "Protect you from what? You're the officer of the court."

"From finding my words quoted in your paper perhaps?" Jake pursed his lips, and eyes squinted, he considered the possibilities. "Or…maybe you're just trying to protect my career."

Mia tossed her head and made a snorting sound as she stared at him. "Now why would I do that?"

"Because you're conscious of the threat to your career, and your brother's, but mainly because you're a caretaker, firebird. You care about others."

This time, her snort sounded louder. "And you know all that from what? The few hours we've spent together? Come on, Judge. Stop channeling Dr. Phil. I need that disc."

The loud rustle of the wind in the trees outside the cabin filled the silence as Jake stared at her. "I need to know why you were in the courthouse the same time the fire started."

Did he doubt her because she was a reporter, or because she had slipped past security to get inside the courthouse? Fingers clenched on the edges of the laptop, Mia demanded. "You don't believe someone shoved me in that closet and blocked the door so I couldn't get out, do you?"

From the chair on the other side of the coffee table, Jake watched every twitch of her expression, every breath. "When you talk about your brother, I hear love. But I hear doubt, as well. Are you afraid of being disappointed by your brother's actions, Ms. Clark?"

How did he know? Could he read her mind? "Haven't you ever questioned some of the decisions your siblings made?"

Jake shrugged. "We are talking about your brother. Do you think he might be guilty?"

"It doesn't matter. Phil is my brother. I love him."

"I can hear the doubt in your tone. If he is guilty as the model claimed, what will you do?" Jake settled back in the chair, waiting for her answer.

"Phil has a responsibility to the family who loves him, and people who elected him to office. I'm praying he told the truth." Chin tilted, she repeated. "Will you give me the disc?"

Jake tossed the purple blob to her.

Heart hammering against her ribs, Mia reached up to catch the small device. Jake hadn't repeated his question about whether she intended to try to erase the disc. Was he starting to trust her? Or maybe he didn't care because he was planning to turn her over to police?

Wanting answers, from the disc and her own muddled questions, she plugged the purple object in the USB drive and held her breath. After long seconds, the screen flickered but remained fuzzy. Pain exploded behind her eyes. All this time, the hope, the risk. Holy cow, the risk, she still couldn't believe she had broken the law and skipped past security. And for what? A big fuzzy nothing on the screen. "It won't open."

Her frustration spilled out as she aimed an accusing glance at Jake. "You knew, didn't you? You tried the disc while I was in the shower." Chest heaving, she gulped air as she said. "Did you erase the disc? Damn you, answer me? Did you ruin my chances of clearing Phil?"

"Who's showing a lack of trust, now, Ms. Clark?" Jake lifted a wide shoulder and frowned. "Look at the disc. It got hot enough to change shape."

Mia stared at the purple disc. He was right. She should have known the instant she saw the strange shape, but she had hoped. "Maybe the techs at the paper can read the disc?"

"Can we risk asking?"

"Risk?" She could feel Jake's eyes on her as she battled with the question. Going to the tech would put another person at risk. It gave someone else a chance to see the ex-model's hidden evidence, but the danger of putting another person in the path of the murderer forced her decision.

"No." She ejected the USB disc. "Here, take it."

Jake met her burning gaze. "It's your evidence, guard it."

"Does that mean you trust me?" Swallowing, she stared down at the screen and rushed on before his answer destroyed the unspoken truce between them. "Do we have internet service here?"

"I doubt it." Jake leaned back in the chair. "It's time you filled in the blanks, Ms. Clark. How is your brother connected to the model?"

Hearing the doubt Jake's voice caused the A-frame ceiling and rock fireplace to close in on Mia, making it hard for her to breathe.

How indeed. It was a good question. But Jake wasn't on the same wavelength with her, obviously. Maybe he didn't mind asking loaded questions. Or maybe her tension came from reacting to the way he looked without a layer of soot on his body. His brown hair glistened with damp from his shower. The new black t-shirt hugged his chest, making his eyes dark as the lake outside the deck.

Sighing in resignation at the danger to her emotions, she faced facts. Jake was a very appealing man. The type of man she wanted to spend her life with.

Clearing her throat, she forced her mind back to his question. "After her modeling career ended, Leigh Anne went to work for the pharmaceutical company." Mia glanced down when the laptop beeped. "No internet service, but I have a file on her."

"Why?"

Mia stared at the screen, hoping he wouldn't notice the color warming her cheeks. "I'm a reporter. Leigh Anne Saddler filed a lawsuit against my brother. I wanted details."

"You must love your brother very much."

Mia stared at him for a few breathless seconds. "You said that before, why?"

"Research takes time. Instead of following leads on a story for your career, you did research to help your brother. That sounds like love."

Or sibling rivalry. She couldn't explain her deepest secret to this stranger. Her family's dynamics might not suit her, but they were her family. Her reasons were none of Jake's business. She shrugged. "I want to find the truth."

Pushing out of the chair, Jake came over to the sofa and sat down beside her. "Show me the file."

Biting her lip to hide her response to his nearness, Mia clicked on the file labeled with the model's name. Good thing she could function on autopilot. Jake's clean male scent and the warmth searing through her body from his arm touching hers, sent her thoughts in a tailspin.

But someone murdered the model, and they were dealing with a life and death matter. Her reaction to Jake was bad timing, but now, she understood the hint of sadness in his eyes. He seemed too young to lose a wife, and she couldn't help but wonder how his wife died.

Teeth clenched, she focused on the file. Leigh Anne Saddle was dead, and she didn't want to be the next victim. She needed to ignore her response Jake.

"Here it is. I researched the drug company, too. The notes are in the same folder." She pushed the laptop over so Jake could read the screen. Her hand brushed his. They were sitting so close, their bodies touched from hip to knee. Awareness flared into a longing so strong she almost forgot about finding the model's body.

Closing her eyes, breathing in the scent of soap and Jake's masculine aroma, she forgot her mother's demands and Phil's troubles. Leaning against the back of the sofa, she sighed. What would have happened if they had met under normal circumstances?

Would Jake have noticed her? Would her insides have tingled when she looked at him the way they were doing now? Would he have allowed her to get close, or rejected her because she was a reporter?

⚲

Jake clenched his jaw as he read the files. Mia Clark was good at her job. He would say that for her. Her files were detailed and long. How much time had she devoted to saving her brother's skin?

He admired determination...and loyalty. He would give anything to have a chance to show his wife an ounce of the loyalty Mia showed her brother. But he couldn't go back and redo the past. He had loved his wife and child and lost them. For the past six years, he existed one day at a time. But it was time to move on. Time to face the life he had now.

He had known Mia only a short time, but she filled a hole he hadn't realized he had in his life. That scared him. Excited him. Who was this woman he was trying to protect? Was she telling the truth? If she wasn't, why?

After uncovering the model's body, he realized Mia's secrets could get them both killed, but he was determined to find out who started the fire, and Mia was his only lead. Yet, honesty forced him to admit there were other factors at play. The heat of her body warmed his side as she curled up next him.

He noticed the innocence on her face as she relaxed in sleep. Washing the soot out of her hair hadn't lightened the color. Dark strands tumbled over the sofa cushion in shining waves. Long lashes curled on cheeks tinted with color from the warmth of the room.

He turned the furnace on when they arrived, and thought of using the fireplace to fight against the chill, but didn't dare for fear of attracting attention to the cabin. He wasn't sure how often Dan used this place during the winter, but he wanted their presence to go undetected.

The more files he read, the more convinced he was of their need to be cautious. Mia's notes named prominent people frequently in the news. If he recognized those names, others would too. Was the connection to the drug company the cause of Phil Clark's trouble?

The names in the file added to the danger Jake had only suspected until now. Even with finding the model's body, he hadn't been certain that Mia was in danger, but after reading her notes, he wasn't going to take any chances.

Big drug company executives had access to mega bucks and could hire their dirty work done. If they were at the root of the model's death, Mia was in danger, and so was he.

He shut down the computer and leaned back against the sofa cushion. Late afternoon sun glistened on the smooth surface of the lake. Tall pines outside the cabin swayed in the wind, making a soothing roar.

Had Phil Clark been close to the model? Was the senator capable of murder? Who murdered Leigh Anne Saddler? Why? Was there a connection to Mia's brother or was this just a strange coincidence?

Until Jake found the answers, he couldn't allow Mia out of his sight. He needed to find out if the ex-model had been the intended target. He couldn't take the risk of calling anyone for information. He needed the internet to find answers.

Some time later, his eyes popped open when something warm nudged his side. He blinked, and realized he had fallen asleep for a couple hours, judging by the darkness outside. The warmth of Mia's body snuggling against his side brought him out of a deep sleep.

But beams of light flashing through the windows brought him to instant alert. He eased away from Mia, pulled on his shoes, and rushed to look out the window facing the drive.

Twin beams of light crept down the twisting drive. Friend or enemy? Even a friend could put them in danger. He didn't know who the enemy was, but the model's body proved them capable of murder.

That left Jake with one option. He had to protect Mia. He brought her here thinking they would be safe. Now, his protective instincts flared. Being an officer of the court didn't matter. He brought her here, and he would do whatever he needed to protect her.

Turning to the bookcase next to the fireplace, he felt along the top of the wooden structure until he found the gun Dan kept there in case of emergencies.

This far out in the woods, danger lurked on all sides, from snakes and the risk of intruders from the lake. Dan had prepared to protect his family and his property. Jake gave a swift word of thanks as he slipped the clip in the Beretta.

Grabbing two extra clips, he stuffed them in his pockets, and headed for the back door. Then he came to a dead stop. Man, there was that word again. The last thing he wanted was for one of them to end up dead like the model. He needed to investigate, but he didn't like leaving Mia alone.

This time of day, the unannounced visitor would expect residents to be inside so Jake switched on a lamp. He glanced at Mia's sleeping form. Waking her to explain the danger would take valuable time. Sound asleep, she should be safe. Convinced this was best, Jake grabbed his jacket and eased out a door on opposite side of the house from the driveway.

His preparations had taken valuable seconds. The vehicle was closer than he expected. Running around the side of the house, he angled toward the driveway entrance. Darkness and dense growth slowed him, but he arrived in front of the house just as the vehicle stopped.

Creeping up behind the SUV parked at the front porch, Jake eased forward in darkness. The only light came from the dim glow of the lamp he left on in the den. An owl hooted in a near-by tree. Sounds from night animals along the lakeshore filled the air. His ears roared with the pounding of his heart and thundering pulse.

A shadowy figure eased out of the dark colored Jeep and looked around. Looking for other vehicles, or waiting for reinforcements?

Jake couldn't tell if the tall figure was armed or alone, as he eased forward, careful not to step on fallen twigs. Armed or not, he couldn't let the man get inside where Mia was sleeping. He thought she would be safe if he confronted the man outside the cabin, but now he regretted leaving her asleep. She was defenseless, alone and asleep in a strange cabin. It was his duty to protect her.

Staying crouched along side of the vehicle, Jake inched forward.

The shadow moved slowly, finally looking under the rock where Jake had found the spare key, then pausing to peep in the front window.

Heart racing, Jake tightened his grip on the gun. Was Mia still asleep? Was she visible from the window? The back of the sofa should protect her if she stayed asleep.

Bending at the waist, ready to rush the man and pin him against the wall, every muscle in Jake's body froze when a screaming yell from the garage blasted louder than the night sounds from the lake. The loud shadowy shape advanced toward the intruder with arms flinging in all directions and waving a long object reflecting light.

At that moment, Jake caught a glimpse of the intruder's face in the beam of the headlights and rushed forward, to fling his body between the man and the frenzied woman ready to attack. "Mia! Stop!"

Mia was two feet away from sticking the long thin blade of a butcher knife in her target when Jake grabbed her arm. "It's Dan. This is his cabin."

"Dan?" Mia sagged against the window at her side, and panted for breath. "Why did you sneak up on us like that? Why didn't you call?"

Struggling for air, Dan leaned against the side of the cabin and stared at them. "I tried."

"I disabled my cell phone." Jake unloaded the Beretta and put the empty gun in his pocket. "I called you from the new phone."

"I was driving slow so I wouldn't alarm you." Dan pushed away from the wall. "Guess that didn't work."

"Sorry," Jake clapped Dan on the shoulder, "we're on edge."

"Let's get inside. You gave me a case of the willies." Dan walked to the Jeep. "I brought supplies."

While they unpacked the groceries, Dan filled them in on the latest news. "The evening broadcast said the dead model was pregnant."

"Pregnant?" Mia gasped and turned wide eyes on Dan. "Do...did that say who—"

"They won't have that information yet," Jake interrupted her wobbling question, giving her a warning glance. It was obvious she suspected her brother, but the fewer people who made the connection, the safer they were. And he didn't want to compromise Dan's safety.

Dan pulled an internet flash disc out of his pocket. "I thought you might need this. Give me the keys to your car. Keep the Jeep."

"Why?" Eyes open wide, Mia stared at the two men. Her voice trembled as she turned to Jake. "We should be okay. No one knows I'm with you."

"The killer knows. He tracked us to the restaurant and slashed the tires." Jake hated that he couldn't answer her unspoken plea for reassurance. "Dan's right. We need to switch vehicles." He turned to the other man. "But that won't work. I don't want your family at risk if you're spotted in Mia's car."

"I figured that out," Dan grinned as he pulled a set of keys out of his pocket. "My dad's place across the lake has a garage. My parents are on a cruise so no one should notice I've changed vehicles. If you need to relocate, you can hide there."

"What about neighbors?" Mia's voice wobbled.

"They have space, but not like this." Dan nodded to the lake. "The development is near the American Tobacco Trail so bicycles are passing all the time, but that's all the traffic you should encounter."

Jake nodded. "We won't go across the lake unless we absolutely have to."

"It's yours if you need a new hiding place."

"We really appreciate this." Jake clapped Dan on the shoulder.

"I'll stash your car in the garage and pump the bike tires." Dan turned toward the door.

"How will you get home if you hide my car?" Mia asked.

"After I stash your car, I'll ride up the trail and call my wife. Tell her I rode too far and got caught in the dark. She'll come pick me up."

"Don't take any chances with safety." Jake ordered.

Dan's grin spread wide. "I won't. This is like being a kid again and playing cops and robbers. I love it."

"Please, don't take any risks." Mia touched his sleeve.

Dan's grin faded. "Don't worry. I tried enough cases in court to know I needed to cover my tracks. Take care of yourselves."

Two minutes later, Dan drove her Honda up the bumpy drive.

🚲

"If she was pregnant…the child might have been a member of my family." Mia paced the great room after Dan left.

"Your brother denied their relationship, under oath."

"You don't know Phil." Chewing on a thumbnail, Mia turned to him. Seeing the honor and justice side of him, she paused. "I'm not sure I believed him." She stared down at her toes. "Phil has always done what he wanted. Winning election to the senate added to his attitude of being entitled."

"Is that why—"

"Okay," Mia plopped down on the coffee table, so close in front of him their knees touched, as she stared in his eyes. "My mother thinks Phil is perfect. She's the one I'm trying to protect. If Phil's career is ruined, it will destroy her."

"You think he was involved with the model?"

Mia shoved off the table and resumed pacing. "Leigh Anne was a secretary for a bigwig at the drug company."

"We're back to the drug company." Jake put his feet to the coffee table and crossed his hands behind his head. "We need to check out Leigh Anne's apartment. See what clues we can find."

"You can't enter a possible crime scene." Mia stopped pacing as she stared at him. "What am I saying, of course you would know that. You're an officer of the court."

Jake got up and turned to the desk in the corner. "I want to know how a body ended up in my courthouse and find a killer."

"What are you looking for?"

"Phone numbers. Addresses." Jake looked up from the phonebook in his hands. "Do you have Leigh Anne Saddler's address in your files?"

Mia opened the computer. "I have a list of employees. Three of them live in the same neighborhood."

"Interesting…is the model one of them?"

"No, she lives…lived in a condo in Durham." Mia watched him put the phone book away and reached to shut down the computer. "Are we leaving?"

Jake stared at her for long seconds. "See if you can find a back-pack in the closet."

Ten minutes later, with two backpacks holding their new cloth-ing items and her computer, they left the cabin. Mia paused at the door. "What about the food Dan brought? Should we clear out the fridge?"

"We'll be back," Jake locked the door and hid the key. "If not, Dan will check on the place."

♾

Tension crawled along Mia's nerves as the Jake eased the Jeep up the crooked drive. Except for the beam of their headlights, eve-rything around them was pitch black. She lived in town. The lack of light and the emptiness of their surroundings added to her dis-comfort. "I want to catch the person who murdered Leigh Anne."

Jake glanced through the dusky interior of the car. "You were after her hide when we met."

"I wanted information. I didn't want to hurt her." Mia swal-lowed the jitters clogging her throat and stared out the window. "I could have been an aunt, again."

"Do you get along with your brother?"

"I love his kids." Mia stared into the darkness and shivered. "No one should get away with taking a life, especially not a pregnant woman and her unborn child."

"If her pregnancy didn't show, the killer might not know." Jake's tone hitched, his eyes glowed in the half-light from the dash. "That's it. We've been looking at this all wrong."

Tension tightened around Mia's chest. "Looking at what?"

"What if Leigh Anne was the intended victim? What if she was murdered because of her pregnancy?"

"Why leave her body in the courthouse?"

"To implicate your brother. It's the perfect crime. Leigh Anne filed charges against Phil, dragging him into court, risking his chances of re-election. Phil is the first person police would suspect of the murder. It is perfect cover for the real killer."

"So Phil didn't murder her?" Mia stared at Jake, her body vi-brating with excitement. "Someone wants him to look guilty, but he's innocent." She released a deep sigh. "But who wanted Leigh Anne dead if it wasn't Phil?"

"The father of her baby? Who could that be? Her boss? A lover? Someone she was blackmailing? Someone from her modeling life? The list is endless." Jake glanced at passing road signs. "Help me watch for the exit."

Chapter Seven

Leigh Anne's address led them to a neighborhood near Center Towne Mall. By the time they arrived, it was so late most of the dwellings were dark. BMW's and Mercedes were parked in the driveways as Jake eased the Jeep down the street. The unit on the end matched the ex-model's address. "Nice area."

"How are we going to do this?" Mia's heart thumped as she stared at the dark building. Computer research she could do, but searching a dead woman's apartment wasn't one of her skills. Dread and tension twisted her insides as she stared at the dark condominium. "Do they have security cameras?"

Jake checked for any sign of security cameras and shook his head. "They were counting on close neighbors and high rent to keep undesirables out, it appears." He eased the Jeep around the circle drive and kept moving. "We'll park on another street and walk back."

"Won't we attract attention?" Mia clenched a sweaty palm around the door handle. "We need a dog."

"The next best thing to walking a dog is pretending to be lovers on a midnight stroll." Jake sent her a glance out of the corner of his eye as he turned of the engine. "Don't worry. We won't go in if we don't like the way things look around her place."

Holding hands, they strolled toward the model's address. The night air carried distant sounds of traffic from a block away on I-40 and chilled her cheeks. A night bird called over faint sound of dogs barking in the distance.

The heat Jake's touch warmed her hand and arm all the way to her shoulder. The contrast of the tingly warmth and the cold night air made her shiver. Who was this man? Why did Jake make her feel safe? Being with Phil never gave her the sense that nothing could happen to her while she was in his company. How could this stranger make her feel safe?

Yet, here she was, risking her reputation and her career for Phil and all she was thinking about was Jake. She smothered the urge to giggle as they approached the back of Leigh Anne's unit. The sliding doors were in deep shadow.

A dog barked from a nearby dwelling. Feeling exposed, Mia inched so close to Jake they made one shadow as they approached the doors. He gave a flick of his wrist. She heard the click of metal and realized he had opened the door. The next instant, he pulled her inside and closed the door.

"Police must have left the door unlocked." Jake whispered against her ear. Cautiously, he checked the kitchen and living room. "Stay close. We may not be the only uninvited guests."

Heart thudding in her throat in response to his warning, Mia checked each shadow for any sign of movement as she followed Jake to a back room she quickly identified as a home office.

Mouth against her ear, Jake said, "Bedrooms must be upstairs. We'll check down here first. Look for address book, diary, anything that might give us a clue."

Mia shivered as the warmth of his breath brushed her cheek. Now she knew why Jake told her to raid the cabin's kitchen for rubber gloves. Tiptoeing to the desk, she started to search. First, she looked in all the drawers and found nothing. Then in the edge of the tiny beam of her pen light, she spotted a laptop on a lounge chair in the corner.

She glanced over to where Jake was searching bookshelves with a pen light and reached for the laptop. In seconds, the screen glowed. Startled by the amount of light the screen gave off, she stared around the room, checking for window, but found none.

Sighing in relief, she turned to the screen in front of her. The list of files on the hard drive was so extensive she didn't have time to check them. Opening the top drawer of the desk, she pulled out one of the stick drives she spotted when she searched the drawer, plugged the disc in and hit save.

"Nothing here, what did you find?" Jake mouthed next to her ear. Something deep in her abdomen twisted in response to his warmth and nearness.

"I copied files." Mia stopped whispering and cocked her head, trying to listen over the thumping of her heart. "Did you hear something?"

A dull thud, sounded overhead. Had someone bumped against furniture upstairs? The hair on her neck quivered. Chills chased down her spine.

Jake moved silently toward the door and motioned for her to follow.

Mia's muscles jerked with tension as she shut down the computer. She was all thumbs in the rubber gloves and tried twice before she managed to remove the disc drive.

Carefully placing the computer exactly as she found it, she joined Jake at the door. "The noise I heard was human."

Jake nodded and took her hand as he headed back down the hall toward the sliding doors.

Heart thundering, Mia stared around the apartment as she followed him. Leigh Anne's taste in furnishings was modern and expensive considering the glass lampshade and large animal print throw on the sofa in the living room.

At the door leading to the kitchen, Jake held a finger up to his lips and leaned his head out to check the staircase. Mia turned to look in the living room. Had that tall shadow been there when they arrived? Had it moved? Did she hear a snapping sound like someone's knees popping?

At that instant, Jake grabbed hold of her arm, pulled her through the kitchen and out the sliding door. Once they were outside, he pushed her against the building into the deep shadows and latched the door. Lips against her cheek, he mouthed, "Get rid of the gloves."

Sucking in a gulp of air, Mia ripped off the rubber gloves and shoved them in her pocket. Teeth clamped on her bottom lip, she struggled to remain calm. If Jake pulled her against his chest one more time, she wasn't going to be responsible for her reaction. Even with her feeling scared half to death, his touch caused heat to pool low in her abdomen, and shivers skated along her backbone.

Desire and fear mingled to form a potent mix inside her.

She was startled back to reality when Jake motioned her to follow him along side the building. At the corner, he took hold of her hand and pulled her from shrub to shrub until they were next to the street. Glancing around to make sure they hadn't been followed, Jake started walking at a speed that took them back at the Jeep in seconds.

He clicked the remote to unlock the doors, and they climbed in. Jake started the engine and headed down the street. "Sorry about the speed walking. One of neighbors might suffer from insomnia and look out the window."

Hot, from the exertion of the past few minutes and her reaction to Jake's touch, Mia filled her lungs with cool night air. What was it about Jake Stone that touched her on this level? She had her share of dates. Dated some good looking enough to be hunks, worked with men who were desirable, and wrote reports on some real dreamboats, but her response to Jake was very different.

What if…

ڴ

Jake glanced in the rearview mirror for the fifth time in the past minute and drove down 751 twenty miles over the speed limit. Twin beams of light followed. Coincidence? Had they picked up a tail? Who?

"What's wrong? You keep looking in the rearview mirror."

Lifting one shoulder, Jake glanced in the mirror again. The vehicle behind them wasn't close enough to light up the interior of the Jeep. "This vehicle has been behind us since we pulled out from Leigh Anne's street."

"This is a well traveled road." Mia glanced at the numerous houses along their route. "Could be someone coming home from work or a movie."

"Yeah."

"You don't think so?" Mia twisted around to look over her shoulder, but all lights looked the same at this distance. "Pull into Dunkin' Doughnuts."

"You want coffee?" Jake tried to keep the incredulous note out of his voice as he wheeled the Jeep into the parking lot at the doughnut shop. Mia had guts. He would give her that. None of the women he knew would have followed him into a stranger's apartment and risk being caught by police.

But he had made the biggest blunder of all.

He should have been more alert before slipping into the model's condo. Five minutes after they entered the condominium, he sensed another presence. He had been listening movement overhead, when Mia heard the thump. He hadn't wanted to frighten her, but they'd had a narrow escape.

Parking at the doughnut shop, he kept his focus on the highway, waiting for the vehicle to pass. Another part of his brain absorbed Mia's presence. How could he ignore her? The scent of her shampoo filled his senses and reminded him of the past.

But Mia affected him on another level, as well.

Her courage and keen intelligence impressed him, but this was neither the time nor the place for such thoughts. Still staring at the highway, he gripped the steering wheel with both hands. It had been six years since he had noticed a woman on this level. Six years. That's how long… "There it goes, a sleek black SUV."

"Is that the car?"

Jake turned to look at her. In the dim light from the doughnut shop, her eyes were large and shadowed. She had tied her hair low on her neck, making her look young and defenseless.

"It's the same shape, and the first vehicle to pass. Considering the time of night, I'd say it was the same one." He watched her nod. "You want coffee and a doughnut? We've got a lot of research to do when we get back."

Mia grinned and reached for the door. "I'll go in. No one around here knows me."

"Hang on a second." Jake put a hand on her shoulder and stopped her. Leaning close, he reached back and pulled the band out of her hair. Her breath caught in a tiny gasp that almost made him forget they were in danger. *Almost.* "Let's change your appearance, just in case."

Looking at him from wide eyes, Mia licked her lips and gave a slight nod. Then she ran her fingers through the dark strands, and sent him a fake smile. "What do you want?"

What do you want?

Jake's gut twisted. He clenched his hands to keep from reaching for her. This wasn't the time. Even if he wanted to take things to a different level, it wasn't fair to Mia.

He hadn't looked at another woman since his wife and son died. His friends thought he was still grieving. People believed he was still in love with his wife. Not one person in his life had guessed that guilt held him prisoner.

He hadn't protected his wife and child when they needed him most. He had no right to put Mia in danger if he couldn't save her. So why had he brought her along tonight? Taken her into an empty condominium? A crime scene no less.

"Tall, brewed, cream, no sugar." He forced the words past stiff lips as if he were speaking to a stranger.

Mia stared at him for a moment longer, gave a nod, and slid out of the Jeep.

Jake scanned the parking area for any sign of danger. He glanced toward the direction the black SUV had traveled, and then watched Mia as she entered the shop.

There was no sign of the vehicle or any hint of danger from the shop, but he knew the danger was inside him. How long could he deny his attraction to Mia?

🚲

Hours later, Mia looked up from the laptop, stretched her arms over her head, and yawned. "We have files on the company executives and their secretaries. What else do we need?"

"How are they connected? Why did Leigh Anne keep these files? What are we missing?" Jake looked up for the legal tablet he was making notes on and leaned back in his chair. He felt as sleepy as Mia looked. Flushed cheeks and her dark hair flared over her shoulders like a curtain of silk, took his thoughts off the murder.

He stood up and tossed the paper down on the coffee table. He would go crazy if he continued thoughts about Mia. He crossed the room to check he had locked the doors, and he forced his thoughts back to the crime. "Get some sleep. We'll get more done after we've had some rest."

Mia looked at him, exhaustion lining her face. "Are we safe here?"

Jake glanced over his shoulder. "I don't see why not. No one knows we're here."

"That car—"

"We don't know if that vehicle was following us. Stop worrying. Get some sleep." He walked over and turned off the light over

77

the kitchen range. The only light left on was the lamp on the table beside Mia. The glow made her hair shine like a halo, but he refused think about...."Tomorrow you need to convince me that your brother is innocent."

Mia clamped her lips. Her chin wrinkled like a prune. The glare she sent him reminded him of his third grade teacher, and he had never forgotten what that meant. *Pain. Punishment. Regret.*

🚲

"Come listen to this," Jake called over his shoulder the next morning when he heard Mia's steps in the hallway. He hadn't slept a wink. She appeared looking flushed and fresh from her bed.

"What—"

"Listen." Jake pointed the remote toward the screen and turned the volume up.

The TV new anchor's voice filled the room. "Police officers arrested Pam Foley this morning around three A.M. and charged her with breaking and entering the apartment of Leigh Anne Saddler. Officials found Ms. Saddle's body two days ago in the charred remains of the Courtney County Courthouse in Pittsboro. Authorities suspect Ms. Foley might have been looking for something that connected her to her co-worker's death."

Mouth open, Mia stared at the images on TV. When the announcer moved on to the next news story, she turned wide eyes on Jake. "They think a woman murdered Leigh Anne?"

Jake studied Mia's shocked expression. "You don't?"

"No, I don't." Frowning, she dropped down on the sofa and raked her hair back with both hands. "You said a woman couldn't carry the body up the stairs in the courthouse."

"Unless Leigh Anne was alive and walked up the stairs."

"Okay, but we were across the hall from the records room. Wouldn't we have heard the attack?"

"Ummm, true," Jake paused, "unless she was already dead when we arrived."

"What was the time of death? Did the announcer say?" Mia looked at him across the coffee table with a hopeful expression in her eyes.

"Nothing on the news about time of death. I could call and find out, but we can't the risk. Police could track our phone."

Mia's eyes widened. "Dan could ask—"

"Officials wouldn't release that information, because he doesn't have connections to the case." Jake held up a finger. "If they got curious and searched for why he was interested, it would lead them to us."

Shoulders slumping, Mia heaved a loud sigh and jumped to her feet. "I need coffee."

"I'll whip up some breakfast." Jake moved past her. "While you tell me what Pam Foley was looking for in the model's apartment."

�🚲

Several hours later, Mia closed the laptop and stared across the coffee table at Jake. She hardly slept any last night. She couldn't stop thinking about Leigh Anne's body, lying in that pile of ashes with her throat slit, and the murderer was following them.

And Jake Stone lying in bed in the next room.

"I can't find anything linking Leigh Anne to Pam Foley other than the fact that they worked for the same company." After hours of combing through Leigh Anne's files, her head ached.

"Then we fall back to plan B. Ask Pam Foley for an interview."

"What plan B? You think she would talk to me? Any way, she's in police custody, remember?" Mia leaned back on the sofa.

"She's made bail by now, and you're a reporter." Jake rubbed a hand over his day old beard. "She'll be glad to talk and I'll go along as your cameraman."

"What camera?" Mia arched a brow. "Do you think she was the one we heard in the condo?"

"Someone there, but it wasn't the secretary."

Mia stared at him. "How do you know? We didn't see who was upstairs."

"Time." Jake tapped his wrist. "Pam Foley was arrested around three A.M. We were back here by twelve. And don't forget some-one followed us."

Mia's imagination supplied the watch he wasn't wearing, but it didn't stop there. The dark hair on his arms made her wonder if he had hair on his chest or if—what was wrong with her? The intruder could have killed them last night. Or they might have been arrested like the secretary had been, but all she could think about was how appealing she found Jake.

"You don't think Pam was the person following us?" She asked, knowing the answer, but not liking it all the same. At least an interview wouldn't be breaking the law. "I'll make the call."

❧

Pam Foley agreed to meet Mia, alone, in a public place. Mia suggested the bookstore at Center Towne Mall in one hour.

Jake stopped at Best Buy on the way and picked up a Flip camcorder. Then they headed for the mall. Arriving early, they entered bookstore from different doors. Jake ordered coffee in the café and picked a seat.

Mia meandered through the store, then stood in line in the café. She ordered two coffees, and chose a seat near enough for Jake to record the interview. Sipping her cup of coffee, she went over the questions she wanted to ask and waited.

Pam Foley approached the table ten minutes later. "Sorry to make you wait but I wanted to be sure you came alone."

Mia swallowed the urge to blurt the truth as the red-haired secretary pulled off dark glasses and a knitted cap. The dark circles under her eyes showed Pam's fear. Keeping her tone friendly, Mia nodded to the table in the corner, near the exit. The redhead had been sitting there when Mia arrived. "I didn't know that was you."

"I have to be careful."

"Is this private enough for you?" Mia indicated their seat near the coffee bar.

Pam shrugged. "I don't see anyone I recognize. I guess this place is as safe. Why did you call me?"

"Are you willing to answer questions about Leigh Anne Saddler?" Mia probed.

"That bitch?" Pam rolled her eyes, stirring the coffee Mia ordered for her so energetically, so sloshed out on the table. "Sorry. I just get so angry when I think—"

"In your place, I'm not sure I could be this brave."

Clamping her lips shut, Pam shook her head. "My lawyer would have a fit if he knew I was talking to you."

"Why did you agree to meet me?" Mia couldn't resist asking.

"Because, I didn't murder Leigh Anne. She was a two-timing bitch, but I didn't kill her."

Mia studied the lines of strain on the woman's face and wondered if she was looking at the face of a killer. "So you weren't friends?"

"We were when she first came to work at Stern-McHamlin, but

Leigh Anne soon made it clear she didn't need female friends. All she cared about was men." Pam glared at Mia across the table. "I can guess what you're thinking. I'm speaking ill of a dead woman who can't defend herself, but every word is true. Leigh Anne dated any VP who asked her out."

"Did that cause tension among the vice-presidents?" Mia swallowed. Could this be the evidence Leigh Anne had hidden? Notes on the company VPs, and nothing to do with Phil? But why claim Phil had fathered her child? Had she lied? "Did she date anyone special?"

"Yeah." Pam's eyes filled with tears and she sat silent for several seconds. "The man I loved for one."

Almost tasting the pain in Pam's voice, Mia passed a napkin for her to wipe the tears streaming down her pale cheeks. "Can you tell me his name?"

Pam scrubbed her eyes and tossed the napkin on the table. "I shouldn't tell you. You probably think, if I really loved him I wouldn't reveal his name and risk getting him in trouble. But I gave him everything for fifteen years, and it wasn't enough. I laid down my life to make him happy. Catered to his every whim at work and after hours," Pam sniffed, and grabbed the napkin again, "well, you can guess what I did after hours. I was in love. Then Leigh Anne Saddler appeared on the scene."

"How did Leigh Anne's arrival change things?" Mia crossed her fingers under the table, hoping the answer to that question would give her reason to believe Phil's claims.

"At first, nothing changed. She was friendly and we got close. Then she guessed I was in love with my boss." Tears streamed down Pam's cheeks. "She started flashing him her model smile and that sexy look she had, and suddenly I found myself with free time at night."

"She went after your—"

"My boss, oh yeah. I may as well tell you. You probably already figured it out, anyway." Pam dabbed at tears. "He thought I wouldn't guess, that I'd back off and watch him go after another woman."

"You caught on?"

Pam nodded her head. "I followed him to a motel. Leigh Anne met him there." Tears streamed down her face. "Silly man didn't even know she was sleeping with someone else at the same time."

"How did you know?"

Pam jerked her head up. Sparks burned in her eyes. "Are you kidding? A woman like Leigh Anne doesn't keep her conquests a secret. Where's the fun in that. If she slept with a new man, she wasn't happy until everyone heard the news."

"Who was the other man?"

Pam clamped her lips and shrugged. "I've said too much already. If my lawyer heard what I've told you he would drop my case."

"I'm not going to the police, Pam. I'm after a story."

"Your story could land me in jail for murder. I've said too much." Pam picked up her hat.

Desperate to stop Pam from leaving before she had enough information; Mia clutched her coffee cup and looked at Pam over the rim. "So, you let her get away with stealing your man?"

"She's dead. What difference does it make, now?" Pam snapped as she prepared to stand.

"It makes a difference here," Mia tapped her head, "and here." She pointed to her heart. "You were used and tossed aside. Why let the past eat at you when you can make things right by telling the whole story?"

Brow wrinkled, Pam settled back in the chair, staring at nothing for long seconds. Then a noisy sigh left her lips. "I don't know the whole story. Leigh Anne got cagey for some reason and stopped bragging. I know she slept with two VPs."

"Which two?" Mia clenched her fingers around the cup in her hand, and held her breath. If Pam clammed up now, she might never discover the truth.

One thousand and one, one thousand and two…

"My boss, Edward Poole, and Charles Herne," Pam's voice clogged with tears. "There was someone else, too, and that senator, but she was welcome to them. All I cared about was Edward. She knew how I felt, that's why she seduced him."

"You're saying there was another man you didn't know? How did you find out?"

Pam shrugged. "Leigh Anne dropped hints about catching a big fish."

"It wasn't the senator?"

Pam laughed. "Phil Clark, not a chance. He was old news. She had some guy she really liked on the hook."

"Any idea who he was?" Mia tried to keep her voice calm.

This might be the lead she needed to clear Phil's name.

Pam shook her head. "She was really into him though, I know that much. So that means he had money and power. Take a guess, that's all I can do."

Shoving back disappointment, Mia toyed with the stirring stick in her cup. "If you had to guess, who would you pick?"

"The two most powerful men at work are Alan Yow and Thomas Goldman, but I don't know if it was either one of them." Pam checked her watch. "I have to go."

Mia felt the urge to hug the woman to offer comfort. Leigh Anne had made Pam's life miserable and now she'd been arrested for plundering the model's condominium. "What did you do when you found out she dated your boss?"

Pam stood and pulled the knitted cap over her head. "I tried to get revenge. I went after Phil Clark and dated Leigh Anne's senator."

Unable to move or breathe, Mia stared as Pam turned away and rushed out the door. Had she heard the woman right? Pam Foley had dated Phil.

After all the time she had spent trying to prove Phil was innocent of Leigh Anne's charges, and he had dated not one, but two women at Stern-McHamlin? How could he do that to his wife and children? To his career? To…oh, no…to mother.

"You don't know that she's telling the truth."

Mia shook her head to break free of the ice freezing in her veins. "She had no reason to lie."

"She knew your name. How hard is it to connect you to the senator?"

"She didn't mention anything about me being related to the senator. She's heart-broken. I could see the pain in her eyes. I feel sorry for her. I don't think she lied."

"We'll check her story. Find out more about Stern-McHamlin and the vice-presidents."

"I'm going to talk to Phil."

"You can't."

Mia angled her chin and glared at Jake. "He's my brother. I'll ask him what I want."

Jake leaned over and whispered for her alone. "We're hiding out, remember?"

Chapter Eight

Mia opened her mouth to argue, then snapped her lips together. How could Phil do this? If he didn't care about his career, what about his family? "Okay, I'll wait but when this is over, he is going to answer my questions."

A muffled scream filtered through the door. People on the sidewalk outside the store started running toward the parking lot.

Mia turned back and stared at Jake. "Pam Foley went out that way."

Without another word, they jumped up and rushed for the door. In the parking lot, they joined the crowd gathering in a dark area, between rows of cars.

"Stay back, people. This is a crime scene." A mall security guard held his arms out to keep people at a distance.

Mia grabbed Jake's arm. "I can't see anything."

"It's a woman," the man in front of them said in a loud voice. "I think she's dead."

Gasps sounded from people near enough to hear the words. Mia's knees trembled. Smoke from someone's cigarette drifted past her nose. Her stomach tumbled. Memories of the stench of burning wood filled her head. She couldn't breathe. Panic almost bent her double. "Jake—"

Jake wrapped his arm around her, pulled her into his body and whispered in her ear. "We don't know it's Pam."

"Sorry, it's…the smoke…what if it is…" Gasping deep breaths

of cold air, Mia managed to stop trembling and forced her body away from Jake's strength. It was so easy to lean on him. But she couldn't. She couldn't get in the habit of depending on him. Look at Phil's betrayal. And her own. If she couldn't be honest about the rivalry with her brother, how could she get involved in a romantic relationship? "The smell of smoke brought it all back."

Afraid someone around them would fit the pieces together, she paused, but she moved away from the man who was smoking. Looking down to watch her step in the dim light, she gasped and almost tumbled to the ground in shock. One-step in front of her, a rainbow stripped cap lay on the ground.

"Careful," Jake moved close and held her arm tight.

Mia stared at him and pointed to the ground as light exploded behind her eyes.

Jake frowned and looked down. "Hell." His head jerked up. His stare bored into hers for about five seconds, then he tugged on her arm. "Come on. We need to get out of here."

Mia stumbled as he tugged her arm. "What—"

"Don't talk. Run."

"Why? Won't the cops think we're guilty or something?"

"Good point," Jake slowed his steps and glanced around. "Keep your eyes open."

"What are we looking for?" Mia twisted her head, searching for the Jeep.

"For the person that killed Pam Foley." Jake held her close to his side as they crossed to where he parked the Jeep. "Someone knew about her meeting with you."

"Oh, no, does that mean the cops will think I had something to do with her murder?"

"Stay calm. The bookstore was so busy. I doubt anyone noticed you were sitting with her."

"Someone did." Mia wanted to believe him, but every time she turned around another body appeared. This time, she might have been the last person to see the murder victim alive. How long before police started searching for her?

⚲

Jake made an effort to keep his speed below the posted limit as he left the mall parking lot. Drawing attention to their departure could bring unwanted interest. At the mall exit, he turned right on

Renaissance Parkway. Keeping a keen glance on the rearview mirror, he made a right turn into the parking lot of a Target store about two blocks away.

"Why are we stopping?" Mia said in a quivering voice. "I want to go home."

Driving to the darkest corner of the lot, Jake backed in a parking space that allowed a view of the entrance and turned off the engine. He wanted to reassure Mia, tell her everything was going to be all right, but the two murdered women proved him wrong.

The next best thing he could think to do was wrap Mia in his arms and hold her tight. But he couldn't even do that. He was certain she didn't have anything to do with Pam Foley's death. She was with him…unless she had an accomplice…how could she? Yet…someone had known they were meeting at the mall.

How? If Mia hadn't told them, how did they find out? Would Pam Foley tell someone who would turn around and murder her? Why would Mia want Pam dead? Because Pam dated her brother? That didn't make sense…unless…Mia had gone to all this trouble for one reason. She wanted to clear Phil's name. Her name, too. Did she want that goal enough to kill the woman who dated her married brother and keep his cheating quiet?

He didn't believe that for one second. But until he had proof Mia was telling him the truth, he couldn't lose control of his emotions. He'd spent every day of the past six years working to pursue justice. Harboring feelings for an arsonist and murder, went against everything he believed in.

Yet, instinct told him that he could trust Mia.

"We'll wait a few minutes to make sure no one is following us." Jake fastened his gaze on traffic entering the parking lot and tried to ignore the woman beside him.

"It's my fault."

Losing the battle, Jake reached across and wrapped his hand around hers. The chill of her skin told him as much about her state of mind as her words. "You didn't murder Pam Foley. But we will find out who did."

"What if the police discover Pam met me in the bookstore? They'll start searching for me. When they can't find me, I'll look guilty."

"Good points. We need to solve these murders fast." Jake

squeezed her hand, then let go to start the Jeep. "I think we're safe. No one seems to be following us. When we get back to the cabin, we'll go over your files on Stern-McHamlin. There has to be some connection to these murders."

"Leigh Anne and Pam were both secretaries to a vice-president. If there's a connection, it has to be something related to the company."

"Or their personal lives." Jake heard her gasp, but after a quick glance in the rearview mirror, he continued. "Both women dated the same two men, maybe more. But that isn't reason enough to commit murder, unless—"

"You think my brother killed them to protect his political career, don't you?"

Ignoring the anger in her voice, Jake checked the mirror as he said. "That's the obvious conclusion."

"Phil didn't—"

"But we need to look beyond the obvious. Thanks to your brother's social activities outside his marriage, he's easy to frame for the murders."

"You mean his adultery." Pain sharpened her voice. "Why don't you just say Phil is a lying, cheating husband? It's what you're thinking. And you're right." She gasped for air. "I can't believe he would cheat on his wife and betray his family."

"If what Pam Foley said is true, and all we have to go on is her word, then your brother is all those things. But that doesn't make him the killer. The big question is why?"

"Why... what? Why did he cheat? I can't imagine. He loves his kids. I thought his marriage was strong, even with his political career making demands."

"Don't stop. Ask yourself, why Pam would say those things if they weren't true?" Jake glanced at her and turned back to the road. Lights glared in his rearview mirror, but he resisted the urge to press the gas pedal to the floor.

"Pam was jealous because Leigh Anne dated her boss, but that doesn't explain why she would lie about dating Phil."

"She hated Leigh Anne for dating her boss. I could hear it in her voice." Jake put a hand to his shirt pocket. "We've got it on tape."

"Pam felt betrayed because she accepted Leigh Anne as a friend. But none of that seems like enough reason to commit murder."

Jake checked the mirror again. The vehicle behind them wasn't passing or falling behind, just keeping pace with their speed. "With Leigh Anne out of the picture, Pam might think she could win her boss's affections again, but that doesn't seem like a motive strong enough to commit murder."

"A woman couldn't have carried Leigh Anne's body up those stairs to the second floor." Mia reminded.

Jake slapped the steering wheel. "We need to get our hands on the corner's report, but that isn't likely if we can't go to police."

"They'll think I'm guilty, won't they?"

"No." Jake frowned and sighed. "Maybe. It will look suspicious when they can't find you. Don't worry. When this is over, I'll explain that I took you into protective custody."

"If we survive, you mean." Mia looked over her shoulder. "That vehicle could have passed any time in the past fifteen minutes, but it just sits back there with the headlights glaring in your eyes."

"Not everyone drives at top speed."

"Take the next exit and see if the car follows us."

Jake shook his head. "I thought about that, but I need to wait until we get to an area I'm familiar with. If the car followed, I don't want to get lost and play into their hands."

"Even if Pam did murder Leigh Anne, who murdered Pam? It wasn't Leigh Anne. And that leaves Phil."

"If Pam isn't the killer, and your brother is innocent, who wants both women dead?" Jake played along with her questions, hoping to ease the tremor in her voice. But the vehicle behind them had him concerned for their safety. He eased off the gas, not enough that Mia would notice, but enough to slow their speed, and still the car behind didn't pass them.

"If we leave Phil out, the only man we're certain the two women had in common is Pam's boss. Both women dated Edward Poole. Both knew he cheated on his wife. What other secrets does he have?"

Jake clenched his hands on the wheel. "What do you know about Edward Poole?"

Mia glanced over her shoulder. "They aren't going to pass, are they?"

If he could reassure her, he would, but they could face disaster any second. Mia deserved the truth. "I slowed down, but they're hanging right behind us."

"If they had a gun, they would have used it by now, don't you think? The road's been empty for miles."

Jake glanced at her. "You think the slasher is in that car?"

"Don't you?" Mia demanded.

Seeing a road sign for the next exit, Jake felt a twinge of relief. There were two more exits before their turn off. If he was going to find out if the car behind was following them, he had to do it now. When the sign for the exit to Hwy 87 appeared, he reached put the turn signal, but jerked his hand back. Why give the car behind notice? "It's now or never."

"Where are we?"

"How adventurous do you feel?"

Mia turned a wide eyed stare on him. "You don't know where you're going, do you?"

"Hang on." Jake took the exit faster than the posted speed. For a second, he thought they were safe. Then the car behind them turned off as well. Muttering under his breath, he made a sharp right turn into a gas station.

"Do you think they will stop?"

"I doubt anyone will try to murder us with witnesses in sight." Jake nodded to the attendants looking out the station windows. "But we'll see."

Two seconds later, the other car passed by the station. Mia let out a loud sigh.

"Don't get your hopes up, yet," Jake warned. "They can't be too obvious or they know we'll call the police."

"W-what if it is the police?"

"It wasn't a patrol car, or a county sheriff's car." Jake frowned as he stared after the vehicle.

"It could be an unmarked car."

"Why follow us? Why not stop us and drag us in if they want to question us?" Jake watched the road for long minutes but the other car didn't return. Keeping a careful watch for any sign of the car returning, he took a left to on Hwy 64 and headed back in the direction they had come.

After two more fake turns, he eased the Jeep off the right exit and drove toward the cabin. Once they were inside, he checked the house carefully, then dropped to the sofa beside Mia.

"This situation is more serious than I thought."

᪙

Two hours later, Jake took a gulp from his coffee mug and grimaced at the cold bitter taste. Cutting a glance to Mia's pale face and drooping shoulders, he leaned back against the sofa with a gusty sigh. "You should get some rest."

Mia turned eyes burning with intensity on him. "How can I rest? I might have caused two women to die, and my brother might be guilty of all the things Leigh Anne claimed?"

She looked so fragile in the dim light from the one lamp they had turned on, Jake wanted to wrap her in his arms and tell her not to worry. But guilt from his past held him back, that and the fact that he knew those words weren't true.

Yet, the urge to comfort her shattered the restraints he usually held on his emotions. He had made those mistakes once before and didn't want to repeat them. He wanted to ease her pain.

Reaching for her hand, he tugged Mia against his chest. Arms wrapped around her, his chin resting on top of her head, he voiced the words they both dreaded. "Do you want to talk about your brother?"

Mia rubbed her head against his shirtfront, making him feel warmer than he had in a long time. Mia was different from women he had dated in the past. In college, he picked the cute, helpless, damsel in distress types. He had loved being a hero for his wife…and their son. But his hero days had ended with the accident that claimed their lives and changed his life.

He wasn't anyone's hero.

He was a judge, sworn to uphold the laws of the land he loved and caught in the middle by his growing feelings for Mia. Should he tell police what he had learned? Or protect the woman in his arms from harm, for he was certain Mia was in the killer's sights.

The vehicle following them tonight had sent that point home.

He couldn't let Mia end up like the other two victims. He had to keep his head clear and his emotions under control. He had to stick to the case, and gather facts. "Tell me about Phil."

Mia toyed with the buttons on the front of his shirt and tried to conceal a sniff. "What's to tell? He was the much loved, first child. The son my parents dreamed of having." Her voice dropped to a whisper. "I always wondered what things would have been like if I had been born first or been a boy."

"That bad?"

"Dad loved me…Mother does too, in her own way, but in their eyes, Phil never made mistakes. Everything he did was right. By the time I reached middle school, that attitude got old and things went downhill from there."

"How so?" Jake ran a hand over the tangled hair on her back, and smoothed it out, because he couldn't resist touching the soft tresses.

Leaning away from his chest, Mia looked in his eyes. "You were in middle school, right?" When he nodded, she rolled her eyes and eased back against his chest. Her next words were muffled against his shirt. "Then you know there are no secrets in middle school. If Phil got in trouble, I heard all the details from classmates. When he told a totally different story at home, I learned to keep my mouth shut."

"You went to a lot of trouble to prove him innocent."

"Phil isn't a bad person, just self-absorbed. But he's my family. I had to help. After all, it's my name he's dragging through the muck, too, you know."

Hearing her sigh, Jake tightened his arms and hugged her closer. The tension building inside him meant trouble if he kept holding her, and he couldn't afford more trouble. One broken heart in a lifetime was enough.

Easing Mia upright, he looked in her eyes with all the determination of a good judge pushing for answers. "Do you think Phil is the killer?"

Mia's lips parted, adding heat to his blood. But the expressions dancing across her face had nothing to do with the awareness building inside him. Doubt, rejection, determination and loyalty flickered across her features, along with other emotions too complicated to identify.

"Never."

Her response came on a gush of warm breath that brushed his cheeks and added to his struggle to keep focused. It was clear Mia didn't hate or resent her brother. Disapprove of his actions and doubt him, maybe, but condemn him for murder, never. This from a sister who knew Phil's weaknesses better than anyone did. Jake trusted her opinion of her brother's involvement.

"Sorry, but I had to ask." He leaned back with a sigh, hating the signs of worry and doubt he saw chasing across her face. "What do we know about Pam's boss, Edward Poole?"

Mia frowned down at her notes and leaned forward to pull the laptop on her lap. "He is vice-president of expansion. Married. He dated Pam and Leigh Anne. Probably owns stock in the company. Tax records show he owns a house on Jordan Lake, a condo at Myrtle Beach and a house in north Raleigh."

"Dating both victims puts him at the top of our list of suspects. I wish we had his phone records."

Mia glanced at his out of the corner of her eye. "Do we have to play by the rules since you are a judge?"

Jake frowned, knowing he wouldn't like what she was about to say. "You don't obey the law?"

Mia lifted a shoulder. "Of course I do. I would lose my job if I didn't—"

"What do you have up your sleeve?" Jake asked. His gut told him he would regret those words, but right now, catching a killer was his main focus.

"If you aren't wearing your judge hat right now, I might know a source who could get us phone records." Mia shrugged, and held her breath as she waited for him to answer.

Jake clenched his jaw for about two seconds. "See what you can find out. Get copies from the other VPs while you're at it."

Blinking in surprise, Mia waited a couple seconds before grabbing the phone. "You know, for a judge, you aren't half bad, Jake Stone."

"Remember those words when you read the head line, Judge Jake Stone, Deposed."

Shaking her head, Mia turned away and punched a number in the phone.

Jake went to the kitchen to get another cup of coffee, relieved he wouldn't hear Mia's words. But his relief didn't last long enough to fill his cup, because a flicker of light in the darkness outside the window caught his attention. Watching the light, Jake held his breath as he waited to see if the light came nearer. Tension building inside him, he willed Mia to hurry up with her arrangements and get off the phone.

By the time she shut off the phone, the light had disappeared, but Jake stayed at the window, watching. Had it been a flicker of headlights from a car passing on the highway? A neighbor out for a stroll? Someone just turning around at the end of the driveway? He considered all the options, but no answers came.

He turned off the coffeemaker and stood staring out the dark window. He saw nothing more, but he couldn't shrug off the sense of danger building inside him. After that vehicle followed them from Durham, seeing a light in the woods was too much of a coincidence. He poured his coffee down the drain, and turned toward Mia. "I'm going outside to check around the house—"

"Not without me, you aren't. Give me second to get my shoes."

Hating to utter the words and add to her worries, Jake met her searching gaze. "Better grab your backpack, as well."

"What is it?" Mia jumped up, on instant alert. "What did you see?"

🚲

Minutes later, Jake led the way and eased through the heavy undergrowth surrounding the cabin. He couldn't risk turning on a flashlight, and unlike the night he had run through the dense growth to get to the front of the cabin to stop the intruder, he couldn't risk making any noise this time.

The other supposed invader had been in a vehicle and couldn't hear if Jake stumbled in the trees. This time he wasn't sure if he had seen headlights or a flashlight, but he sensed danger and to make things even worse, he agreed for Mia to come with him.

He'd left her unprotected in the cabin once. He would not leave her again. That meant double the chances of stepping on twigs or stumbling and alerting the intruder. But he needed her near so he could watch over her.

Mia tugged on his sleeve. When he turned, she put her cheek against his and whispered in his ear. "I don't see anything."

Jake lifted a finger to his lips. He couldn't have said a word if he had tried. The soft warmth of her cheek against his and the clean scent of her hair invaded his senses, sending all sorts of longings racing through his body. Thoughts that could get them killed. He needed to focus on the danger waiting in the darkness, not this growing awareness of Mia that almost crippled him with need.

Moving forward, hoping to shut out the growing warmth in his gut, he aimed for a roundabout route toward the area where he spotted the light. Under the cover of darkness, they searched each shadow, stopping for long moments to listen, and then moving on.

Deciding he had overreacted, that he had blinked or imagined the light, he stopped to assess their location. Leaning close to Mia, steeling his body against the warmth as he brushed her cheek, he whispered. "I don't see anything. It must have been a car going down the road. We should head back—"

"No! Wait," Mia grabbed his arm and whispered against his ear. "I need a light."

"What is it?" Jake went rigid at the sound of tension and fear crackling in her words. "Did you hear something?"

Shaking her head so hard her ponytail brushed his face, Mia whispered against his ear. "I smell smoke."

"What—I don't see any sign of a fire. It's your imagination and the dark. We're okay."

Mia tugged his wrist and pulled the flashlight out of his pocket. Kneeling on the ground, keeping her hand cupped around the lens, she flipped the light on. The tiny beam landed on three new cigarette butts. Mia gasped and almost toppled backwards in her effort to flee from the implied threat and turn the light off at the same time.

A curse escaped Jake's lips. Muscles alert, ready to attack, he scanned the deep shadows around them, but Mia's soft gasping breath was the only sound he heard. After long seconds of searching and waiting, he relaxed enough to pull her into a clumsy embrace. They huddled there, crouched on the cold ground, as close to each other as possible.

Mia leaned into Jake's warmth, but the odor of smoke almost made her gag. The stench of the cigarette butts stirred memories of being trapped in that burning building. But this time, her sensitivity to smoke might save them from a killer. "We need to take these butts as evidence."

Jake kept his eyes on the woods around them, searching for any sign of movement. "I don't have gloves or a plastic bag."

"I do," Mia pulled the kitchen gloves out of her pocket and carefully picked up the cigarette butts. "It's not perfect, but it works."

"Hurry. We need to move. We can't go back to the cabin." Jake mouthed close to her ear. As soon as she finished tying the butts in the fingers of the glove, he urged her into motion.

Moving one-step at a time, checking the shadows the best he could in the pitch-blackness of the tall pines, Jake worked his way toward the lake and Dan's boathouse. Hampered by darkness and the need to stay quiet, he pushed and tugged until he finally managed to free Dan's canoe from storage.

With Mia's help, he eased the small craft in the water without a splash. Securing the oars, he grabbed life jackets from the chest Dan used for storage, and helped Mia into the canoe. With one last glance over his shoulder, he settled on the seat in behind her, and cursed silently at the brightness now that they were out of the shelter of the trees,

Leaning over Mia's shoulder, he whispered. "We can't go very far out on the lake. Our silhouettes will be visible in the moonlight. We'll stay in the shadows close to shore until we get some distance away."

Mia nodded and tightened her grip on the sides of the canoe. She wasn't fond of water, and avoided riding in boats, but staying in the woods with a killer wasn't an option.

Jake had maneuvered the craft only a few feet from the boathouse when a long dark shadow loomed over them from the pier. Mia gasped aloud. Jake swore under his breath and rowed with all his strength to get away. But the shadow kept coming, looking ten feet tall from where Mia sat in the canoe. Horror stole all the air from her lungs as the shadow reached the end of the dock and lunged through the air toward them.

Heart thumping against her ribs, Mia watched the floundering shadow fall in the lake, and the the next instant, hands reached up to grab the side of their boat. But Jake's strength and skill with the oars sent the lightweight canoe gliding out of the reach of the desperate hand of the swimmer.

Many yards later, after she had filled her lungs with air, Mia twisted to look over her shoulder at Jake. Forcing words from her stiff lips, she said. "Should we go back to make sure he didn't drown?"

"And give him another chance to drown us?" Jake grunted as he pulled against the oars.

"You think it was a man?"

Jake leaned forward, resting his arms on his thighs and murmured, "Don't talk. Sound carries on water."

After what seemed a life time, but in reality was only about two hours later, with dawn breaking along the eastern skyline, a friendly angler in a powerful motorboat gave them a tow to the opposite shore. Jake dropped the tow rope, waved to the boatman and rowed the canoe toward the dock.

Mia glanced over her shoulder, searching for any sign of movement on the lake. "Are we safe?"

"I think so." Jake paused to row another stroke. "Even if there was a second person on land watching us, he doesn't know where we landed on this side of the lake."

"Do you?"

Jake eased the canoe in line next to the wooden dock.

Mia held tight to the boards, while he climbed out, and turned to offer her a hand. Tossing him her backpack, hoping her laptop was cushioned; Mia accepted his hand and climbed out. Her legs trembled. The dock swayed. Conceding defeat, she plopped down on the heavy wood boards and drew in a shaky breath.

Jake dropped to the boards beside her. "You okay?"

"Water legs," Mia muttered. He barely seemed winded after all that rowing. "What now?"

"We look for signs, then Google map our location."

"That's your plan?" Mia demanded incredulously. "What if the killer finds us first?"

"Not likely. There are miles of lakefront, besides he'd have to drive to get here." Jake fiddled with his phone and sighed. "I don't know much about this side of the lake, but I think we're close to Dan's parents' house."

Fifteen minutes later, with the help of Google Maps and a brisk walk, they found the house and used the key Dan had given them.

Inside, they found a note from Dan, and more supplies in the kitchen. Hunger satisfied, they showered and changed clothes. Then settled in to watch the early morning news.

Police weren't saying much about Pam Foley's death.

"Center Towne Mall's public relations staff probably squelched some of the headlines." Jake offered.

"Police are looking for a woman of interest to question." The announcer said. "Sources reported seeing the victim talking to a dark haired woman in the bookstore a few minutes before the body was discovered."

Sick to her stomach, Mia turned to Jake. "They think I had something to do with the murder."

"Not necessarily. They just need to track her whereabouts before she died."

Choking back tears, Mia stared at the TV. "I have to meet my source at eleven."

Chapter Nine

The meeting place Mia arranged with her source for the phone records was a cafe, famous for delicious burgers, located on a corner, overlooking the old city baseball park. Small businesses lined the intersecting street.

Ten minutes after they arrived, Jake realized eating burgers as this cafe, meant standing in line and waiting, if the line curling around the building was anything to judge by. Turning to Mia, he voiced his concern. "Are you sure this is the best place to meet?"

"The best part about meeting here is sitting outside. You can see everything." Mia motioned Jake to follow her after they picked up their order.

Patrons sat at long wooden picnic tables under a shelter to eat their burgers. Mia sat down at the end of the only vacant table and waved a hand as she put three bags with their order in the center. "Mmm, this smells so good."

Jake set three tall drinks on the table and sat on the bench opposite her. "You think we missed your contact?"

"Nope." Mia carefully arranged a drink and a bag of food on the end of the table next to her and pushed another bag across to Jake. "Eat and tell me what you think."

Unwrapping the burger in her bag, she took a bite, closed her eyes and sighed. "I am starved."

Jake rolled his eyes, but the first taste of his burger chased all doubts from his head. Either he was starved, or this was the best burger he had ever tasted.

"Well?" Mia demanded when she could speak again. Half her burger had disappeared and she was munching fries. "I told you this was a good idea."

Watching Jake, waiting for him to agree with her, she sighed again and this time it had nothing to do with food. Even with a two-day beard and odd mix of clothing, Jake looked as yummy as the cheeseburger in her hand. His rare smile melted her insides like the cheese on her burger. Strange as it seemed, she felt close to him as if they were old friend, yet she hardly knew anything about him. "You never said. Do you have brothers and sisters?"

Jake eyed her thoughtfully and swallowed. "No and after hearing about your sibling, I'm not sure I missed anything."

Regret washed over her, dulling her appetite. Laying the rest of her burger on the wrapper, she wiped her fingers on a paper towel from the roll in the middle of the table. "We had fun when we were little kids."

"What went wrong?" Jake picked up a fry and munched.

"I—"

The bench shook as someone dropped down beside Mia. She fought to keep her gaze on Jake as if nothing had happened as she continued. "Our teen years hit, I guess."

After giving the newcomer a startled glance, Jake caught on to her act and played along. "Teen years are tough."

Out of the corner of her eye, Mia caught a glimpse of hands unwrapping the third burger she had ordered. "I guess. We never recovered after all the bickering."

"Yo," a gruff voice sounded past a mouthful of burger, "who's the boyfriend?"

"He's safe, don't worry." Mia kept her eyes on Jake as she picked up her drink. To anyone observing them, she and Jake looked like a couple sharing the table with a stranger. They should be safe from spying eyes.

The guy beside her lifted the hem of his over-size sweatshirt and pulled folded sheets of paper from his waistband. In a swift move she would have missed if she hadn't been expecting it, he reached for her empty burger bag, stuffed the pages in like discarded trash, and tossed the bag back on the table in front of her.

"Take care. You're being watched," he mumbled as he grabbed

his empty bag, wadded it up and tossed it in the trash. His drink in one hand and munching the burger in the other, he sauntered away.

"Can you see anyone following him?" Jake asked.

"Not without being obvious and turning my head." Mia slipped the papers out of the bag and tucked them under her sweatshirt as she chew on another French fry.

"I'll check." Jake stuffed his napkin and the wrappers in the bag and stood. Strolling toward the trashcan, he looked around casually as he tossed the bag in the barrel.

Her eyes on Jake, Mia didn't notice the arm reaching over her shoulder until a hand grabbed her burger bag, shoved her sideways, and whirled away.

"Hey," Mia cried as she tried to regain her balance and get a look at the intruder at the same time. But all she saw was the bottom of his athletic shoe as he raced around the back of the building.

Jake heard Mia cry out, and whirled around in time to catch a glimpse of the hooded figure running away behind the cafe. Cursing under his breath, Jake rushed toward her.

An employee appeared at Mia's side. "Miss, are you all right?"

Mia smiled as she turned to the man wearing a cafe apron and carrying extra paper towels. "Thanks, but I'm fine, just clumsy. I almost fell off the bench."

"Are you sure?" The man insisted. "Some woman said a man in a hood pushed you."

Eyes wide, Mia looked up at Jake. "Darling, please tell him I have two left feet."

"Which means I get to pick her up a lot. But that's always fun." Jake wagged his brows in a comical way. The employee laughed as Jake moved to Mia's side. "Let's get you home, sweetheart. You haven't been drinking have you?"

Mia jabbed his side with her elbow as he urged her toward the car. "You'll regret that remark. Hurry."

"Slow down. We've attracted enough attention." Jake glanced over his shoulder, pretending to check traffic, but he didn't see anyone following them. "Give me the keys. I'll drive. Did he get the phone records?"

Mia hesitated a second, then pulled her car keys out of her jeans pocket, making the papers in her waistband crackle. "A minute earlier and he would have. It was a man, wasn't it?"

Jake turned on the ignition and checked traffic. "Hard to tell. I couldn't see much."

"Is anyone following us?"

Jake heard the tension in her voice and winched. He wanted to reassure her, but he couldn't. Two vehicles had pulled out behind them. "I'm heading for the mall. Can you look at those phone records?"

Two blocks later, Jake was confident they were being followed.

Keeping one eye on the highway and checking in the rear-view mirror, he considered their options. But they were out of choices. They were in the Honda Dan had hidden in his parents' garage. If someone had discovered their change of vehicles, they were in more danger than he had thought.

"Edward Poole called several numbers consistently."

"Anyone you know?" Jake watched as the vehicle, two cars back, made the same turns he made.

"Two of the other VPs, Pam, Leigh Anne and Phil." Mia snapped her head up and stared at him. "I know what you're thinking, but Edward Poole is the man who invited Phil to that dinner. He introduced Phil to Leigh Anne, so it makes sense he called Phil's number."

"Relax," Jake whipped the steering wheel to the right, turning down a side street. *Yeah, right. Relax.* They were two steps away from a murderer and he needed to protect Mia. "I'm not saying your brother is guilty. Just give me the facts."

"It's hard to read with you going this fast. How much further?"

As long as it takes to lose the person on our tail? "Not far, I thought this was a shortcut, but it's not."

Mia held on to the dash and stared at him with wide eyes. "Is someone's following us?"

Jake clenched his jaw and made another quick turn. The car was still there. "Hard to say, but I think you could be right."

A quick turn off a side street at the next corner brought them out on Hwy 751. Center Towne Mall was a mile away. The mall was their best chance of losing the person following them.

He glanced at Mia's white face. "I may have to park more than once to lose this guy. When I say the word, jump out and head for the bookstore."

"Are you sure?" Mia darted a look over her shoulder. "We went there once. If it's the same person, he'll know where we're going."

"Right, but it's the only place I can think of with doors on two sides."

Mia opened her mouth and turned wide eyes on him. Jake saw the hint of amusement in her eyes, even with trouble on their bumper.

"Don't even go there. I know those lingerie shops have two doors, but I would stand out like a sore thumb in one of those stores. It's the bookstore, or nothing."

"Then what?"

Jake heard her voice quiver, but she kept her chin high. He admired her courage. He admired many things about Mia Clark. When this was over, he would miss spending time with her. If they made it out of this alive…

🚲

"There's a spot, across from the Italian restaurant." Mia pointed.

Jake wheeled past the trees planted in the median, turned in the parking lot and glanced in the mirror. "The same car is still behind us."

Mia stared out the back window of the Honda. "The black SUV? The windows are tinted so dark I can't see the driver."

Jake rolled past the vacant parking space.

Mia watched him glance in the rearview mirror and guessed he was searching for a chance to elude the car behind them. She grabbed on to the edge of her seat with both hands and held tight. Several twists and turns later, an elderly driver in an older, boxy sedan barely missed hitting the Honda in the side and pulled out in front of the car chasing them.

Taking advantage of the mini-traffic jam, Jake pressed on the gas. "Change of plan. When I park in front of the department store, run for the door."

"If we run, won't that draw his attention?"

"With a little luck, we'll get in the door before this guy spots our car and figures out we're on foot." Jake wheeled in a parking spot and stopped the car. "Let's go."

Clinging to the backpack, Mia jumped out, and dashed over the concrete median and in the front entrance of the upscale store.

Jake followed on her heels. But once they were through the glass doors, he grabbed her hand and pulled her to a stop. "Wait here a second. Let's get a look at this guy."

Camouflaged by the heavy tint used on the glass wall to protect the merchandise, they watched for the vehicle that followed them. Seconds later, a black SUV slowly rolled though the lot. When it stopped behind her Honda, Mia gasped. "Can you see the driver?"

"No, but we're going to wait him out."

"How," Mia demanded. "We don't even know what he looks like." She stared at the rear window of the SUV as it circled out of the lot. "Come on, let's follow that car."

Jake looked at her as if she were crazy. A second later, he grabbed her hand as they ran out the door. As they reached the Honda he said. "Keep your eye on that vehicle."

Mia stared after the black SUV until Jake started the car, then she jumped in and said, "It's in the second lot over, almost to the exit."

Jake reversed out of the parking spot, turned left, and picked up speed. "I see it."

For the next few minutes, they eased through the huge parking areas around Center Towne Mall. When the black SUV stopped, Jake slowed. When the black vehicle moved forward, Jake picked up speed. After they circled the lot twice, he sighed. "The driver must have spotted us."

Mia kept her eyes glued to the SUV. "Why do you say that?"

"Why keep circling the lot...unless...he might be waiting for reinforcements." Jake slammed his hand on the steering wheel. "I should have thought of that. We played right into his hands by following him. When his friends arrive, we'll be outnumbered."

"What now?"

"We don't know where he's leading us. It's time to change the game." Jake slowed the Honda. The SUV pulled away.

"Maybe he didn't recognize the car like we thought." Mia frowned, remembering the SUV stopped behind her Honda in the parking lot. "Go faster. Make him run."

"It's risky."

"If that's the killer, we need to get a description." Mia gripped the door handle. "Speed up. He's getting ahead of us."

The parking area at Center Towne Mall is divided into several small lots with trees planted in the strips separating the parking area from entrance ramps from surrounding highways. As Jake drove across the second entrance road, the black SUV popped out from behind the trees and pulled close to their rear bumper.

Hands gripping the wheel, Jake glanced at Mia. "This can't be good."

"My fault. I lost track of him." She stared straight ahead. "What do we do now?"

"Try to lose him again."

Mia held her breath as Jake darted between two cars leaving the lot. Horns blared. Tires screeched. When she glanced back, the SUV had lost two car lengths. "That helped. My heart stopped, but we gained a lead."

"Not enough." Jake swung the Honda around a tight corner and turned in a lot near a sports themed restaurant, but the area was blocked for valet parking. Jake swore under his breath and said. "Hold on."

Mia gasped as he aimed the Honda straight for the rope barrier.

Jake drove through the rope. Metal posts holding the rope, clanged against the side of the car. One end of the rope whirled in front of their eyes like a cowboy's lasso, before falling to the ground. Pressing on the gas, Jake headed toward the wrap-around road that circled the mall.

Mia looked back. The SUV was nose to nose with another vehicle, at the entrance to the valet parking. "He had to stop for another car."

Jake floored the gas pedal and headed back toward the department store's entrance to the mall. "We need to ditch this car."

🚲

Jake parked in a different spot and stopped the car. He jumped out and Mia ran to keep up with him as they headed to the entrance to the department store. Once they reached the door, she gasped. "We should buy new shirts."

Jake held the door open for her. "Good thinking, but we stay together."

"You first." Mia stayed by his side as he led the way to men's department. They should be safe in the busy store, but not knowing what the person following them looked like gave her chills. "Buy this one."

105

Jake looked at the bright green shirt and shook his head. "May as well paint 'here I am' on my back. We need to blend in."

Mia put the shirt back on the rack. The color matched Jake's green eyes, but his comment brought the danger back in focus. "You're wearing black. Black blends, why change?"

"Humor me," he picked out two black t-shirts and paid the clerk. "Let's go to the women's department."

Heat chased along Mia's limbs as he touched her arm, making alarms go off in her head. Jake would get plus marks as an escort, especially in the dangerous situation they faced. She was happy to have him at her side. Thoughts of fun time spent with him chased through her head and she tried to pull away from his touch. She couldn't think about her feelings for Jake until they were out of danger.

"How about this one?" She pulled a black shirt off the first display they passed in the Ladies' department.

Frowning, Jake put the shirt back. "That neckline would show your navel."

Laughter gurgled close to the surface as Mia stared in his eyes. When this was over…

"I thought you wanted me to wear black."

Ignoring her needling, Jake stopped at another display. "Navy will do."

Two navy shirts in hand, Mia stepped up to the counter and reached for her credit card.

Jake stopped her with a hand over hers and whispered. "Cash only. I'll take care of this."

Heat crawled up her neck as Mia stood by his side while he paid for the shirts. When he turned to walk away, she fell into step beside him. "Guess I failed undercover work 101."

Sending her a glance out of the corner of his eye, Jake shrugged. "I hope you aren't going to make a habit of this type of activity."

Teeth clamped on the inside of her cheek, Mia struggled for a new topic. "Where are we going to change shirts?"

"Food court," Jake said as he steered her toward the escalator, "we can mingle in the crowd while we wait. Oh, look…stop here."

They were outside a beauty salon with hair products and wigs in the window. Mia frowned. "You want me to get my hair cut?"

"Too drastic," Jake pulled her toward the entrance. "I think something temporary." He led the way to a display of wigs. "How would you like going blonde?"

Mouth open, Mia started to refuse, but she saw the challenge in his glance and decided to play along. Ten minutes later, she walked out of the shop wearing a short blonde wig. The pixie style made her feel daring and different. "You should have a wig, too."

With a hand on her arm, Jake turned her toward the food court. "I don't think that's necessary."

"We're trying to change the way we look." Mia batted her eyes at him in a flirtatious manner. "You look the same."

"I took off my cap." Jake nodded toward the food counters. "What do you want to eat?"

She opened her mouth to say nothing, but her stomach growled. "Pizza."

Ten minutes later, pizza and drinks on a tray, Jake led the way to a table near the restrooms. "You change first."

In the bathroom, Mia changed into the navy shirt and washed her hands. A glance in the mirror stopped her as she turned toward the paper towel dispenser. Was that her reflection? The feathery blonde wig made her look like a different person.

Did Jake prefer blondes? Stop.

Forcing her attention away from her image, she snapped to alert and reached for a paper towel. This was not a game of dress-up. This was real. They were hiding from a killer. With that thought, she rushed out to join Jake.

He stood the instant she appeared. "Eat. I'll be back in a second. If anything upsets you, bang on the door."

Biting into the slice of pizza, Mia kept her eyes on the crowd. Chill bumps popped on her arms as she watched strangers eat their food. Would the person following them recognize her? She remembered the wig. She should feel safe, but fear had followed her like a shadow ever since someone shoved her in that closet.

"How are you doing?"

The sound of Jake's voice jerked her out of the depressing thoughts. She glanced at him and gasped. He had slicked his hair back and put on black framed glasses. "I wouldn't know you in a crowd."

Not true, she realized, as his shoulder brushed against hers, causing her heart to thump.

"We forgot one thing." Jake leaned over, took the backpack off the chair beside her, and stuffed it in the large shopping bag between their chairs.

"So, that's why you asked the clerk for a large bag when you bought the shirts." She reached for her drink with a trembling hand. *Was she reacting to Jake, or the situation?* "Should I pull out the phone records?"

"Not here." Jake glanced around. "We don't want to give away our disguise."

"You look so different I doubt there's any chance of being recognized." Mia tore her gaze away from the deep green of his eyes in the black frames. "What now?"

"I called Dan. He's bringing a different vehicle." Jake picked up his drink. "But now, I need a new phone."

Chapter Ten

Staring at the crowd in the food court, Mia sighed. "None of this seems real. I write articles and research information on computer. How did I get caught up in a murder drama?"

"You wanted to clear your brother's name." Jake nodded toward the half-eaten slice of pizza on her plate. "Nibble on that pizza so we don't attract attention."

"How long do we have to wait?" She plucked a pepperoni slice off the pizza and popped it in her mouth.

"Dan gets off work at five." Jake held up a hand when she frowned. "The good news is he can help us."

"A killer is on our trail and we waste the afternoon at the mall?"

Jake gave her a long look. One corner of his mouth lifted in a grin. "Your reaction to an afternoon at the mall is different from any female I've ever known."

Heart thumping, Mia stabbed the pizza with a fork. "You've known a lot of females?"

Hunching a shoulder, Jake stared in the distance. "A few."

"Anyone special?" Mia clamped her lips to keep from asking more. She wanted to know everything about him. What made him tick? Did he have someone special in his life? Someone he loved? But they didn't have that kind of relationship. They were strangers, thrown together in a dangerous situation. She doubted he would answer even one question.

"I loved my wife."

Desperate to hide her shock that he'd mentioned her, Mia picked up the pizza with hands that trembled and took a bite. Chewing gave her time to think. Time to wonder why he used past tense. *Loved.* Finally, her curiosity won. "What happened?"

"She died in an accident."

Tiny bursts of light exploded in front of Mia's eyes. She blinked. "I'm sorry—"

"It was a long time ago."

"Still, you—"

"She and my son were killed by a drunk driver." Jake spit out the words like poisoned darts.

And each one made a direct hit to Mia's heart. He had loved and lost. Been married, been a father and now his family was gone. "I'm so sorry."

Remorse washed over her as she thought about her life. How had she sunk to this level? How had she lost faith in her brother? She had forgotten how much she loved Phil until thoughts of being killed forced her to think of the people she loved. Of course, her mother loved her only son. Mia loved him too. She always had, even before their father died.

Trembling, she blinked as memories filled her head. Everything had changed after her father died. It was more than just the loss of the man they all loved. His death left a gap in their lives and in their relationships with each other.

She could see that now. Could see all her family had lost. The closeness, the unquestioning love, and their sense of family. Had Jake felt the same emptiness? The same loss? She risked a glance in his direction.

He stared in his drink cup, then finally answered her question. "Life happens."

"D-do you want to talk?"

Brow arched, he sent her a sidelong glance. "You mean, we have the afternoon to kill, and you don't have anything better to do than listen to my life story?"

Nostrils flaring, she bit back an angry response. The expression in his eyes showed his pain, and the last thing she wanted was to add to the emotions tearing at his control. She knew that feeling. Blinking moisture from her eyes, she offered an apology in voice that sounded as if she had a cold. "My family fell apart when my dad died."

After a startled glance at her, Jake's shoulders slumped. "Yeah, it happens."

She recognized the pain, regret, and sense of loss echoing in his words. Swiping the corner of her eyes with the back of her hand, she blurted out the first words that popped in her head. "I am so ashamed."

Jake's look of surprise changed to a frown. "After all you've done the last two days to clear your brother's name? You don't have anything to be ashamed about."

Lifting a paper napkin to blot her eyes, Mia sniffed. "I did all those things for the wrong reasons." Tears pooled in her eyes again. "I love my brother, but he changed. I guess we all did. When Mother insisted I find proof to clear his name, I saw the chance to show her Phil wasn't perfect."

"You have risked your life more than once in the past few days. In my opinion, that proves your love for him. There's no reason for regret."

Heat warming her face, Mia opened her mouth to say, *Thanks.* But entirely different words tumbled out her mouth. "Do you have any?"

"Every minute," brows knit, Jake traced lines on the table with his fork. "It was my fault Sara was driving the car that night."

Mia placed a hand on top of his. "You blamed yourself all this time?"

For long seconds, neither of them moved, then Jake turned his hand over and gripped hers. Lifting his gaze, he stared into her eyes. "Same as you have done since your dad died."

"How do you know—"

"You blame yourself, thinking you should have done something different."

Fingers gripping his hand, she didn't need to ask what he meant. She knew. Lowering her voice to a whisper, she asked the question burning in her head. "Could you have changed anything?"

"If I say no, it sounds like I blame her. If I say yes, I'm making an excuse." He shrugged and pulled his hand away. "It's time to face facts. Life happens."

"That's why I can't let the person following us win." She straightened her shoulders. "I intend to clear my brother's name and prove my mother's faith in him isn't misplaced."

And prove I love him. I can't forget that.

Jake looked in her eyes for long seconds. He could almost hear the ticking of a clock as images of his life flashed in his head.

Was Mia right? Could letting go of the past be this simple? Let the memories go and focus on the future?

For the first time since his family died, he wanted a new start. Taking a deep breath, he said, "We have two dead secretaries, a list of computer files, phone records for the vice- presidents, and your brother's motive for wanting the model out of the way. That's a lot of dangling threads and no definite trails."

Mia leaned close so she wouldn't be overheard. "I'm convinced someone is framing Phil."

Jake arched a brow.

Lifting her hand, Mia ticked off points on her fingers. "Both dead women work for Stern-McHamlin, so do the men mentioned in the files, and Phil met Leigh Anne through one of the company's vice-presidents."

Jake frowned and leaned so close, his shoulder brushed hers. "We've hit a brick wall. We can't get inside the company."

"We go through Leigh Anne's files."

"You did that—"

Mia didn't let his reminder faze her. "We didn't know what we were looking for at that time."

"And we do now?" Jake's forehead wrinkled.

"We look for connections to tie these men to a crime."

"In other words, we don't have a thing—"

He stopped midsentence and stood. Grabbing the shopping bag in one hand and her elbow in the other, he urged her out of the food court. "We have to leave. Don't look back, just act like we're shopping."

"What did you see? Where?" Mia's heart pounded in tune with her feet smacking the shiny tile floor.

"Someone wearing a hooded sweatshirt, about five tables over. Could be nothing." Jake walked faster.

"What made you suspicious?" Mia gasped, trying to keep up. "We're going too fast to look like shoppers."

"You're right." Jake slowed. "Don't panic. Pretend we had an argument and we're making up." He stepped in front of her and pulled her against his chest. Lowering his head, he whispered so close his lips brushed hers. "Hold still. I need time to check behind you."

Hold still? Was he out of his mind? A killer was on their trail and Jake's lips were on hers, and he wanted her to stand still?

Mia clutched his shirt in both fists as she stared up at his face. Heat raced through her body. Her heart hadn't beat this fast since she escaped the closet at the courthouse. The need to survive urged her to stand motionless, even as her body begged her to lung forward for his kiss.

"Do you see anything? Is he following us?"

"I can't tell," Jake murmured against her cheek. His breath sent chills chasing along her spine and sent her heart into overdrive. "I need more time to watch."

Abruptly, he lowered his head and his lips brushed hers.

The first touch of his warm lips on hers made her head spin. Who was she fooling, no way could she wait until this was over to show her feelings for Jake. Closing her eyes, she fought for one last shred of sanity to prove she hadn't lost all sense of reality. A little voice shouted in her head, reminding her she wasn't supposed to enjoy this. Jake was checking to make sure they weren't being followed, nothing more. She knew that. Her brain accepted it, but some part of her had other ideas. She sighed and leaned against his chest, offering her lips for another kiss.

Wait. She couldn't.

Reality hit. She forced her eyes open. Jake's lips were sampling hers as if she were his favorite feast, but his eyes watched people behind them. Mia pushed back. If she wanted to get out of this without a broken heart, she needed to remember they were strangers, trying to survive. Nothing more. She gulped. "See anything?"

Cupping her cheek in his hand, Jake stared deep in her eyes. "Wow. That was good acting."

"You said pretend we'd had a fight. Making-up is usually hot." Mia swallowed the lump in her throat and prayed she was a good actor. "What do you see?"

A smile tilted one corner of Jake's lips as he looked down at her. If Mia hadn't been on alert, and known she had to keep her emotions out of this, she might have missed his swift glance behind her. But she was alert and didn't miss his keen glance. Instead, she faced facts. They were fighting for their lives. Jake's words were the reminder she needed.

"I can't be sure. I caught a glimpse of a covered head, but the person turned into a store."

"So either he isn't following us, or he saw us stop and needed cover." Mia realized she was still clutching Jake's shirt in her fists. Forcing her fingers to let go, she took a step back. "What now?"

Hand on her elbow, Jake urged her forward. "We head for the escalators in the center of the mall. We'll watch from there while I make a call."

At the escalators, Jake pulled out his phone. Mia leaned against the waist high rail. Clutching the shopping bag to her chest, she stared past Jake's shoulder and watched behind him.

Phone to his ear, Jake said, "Talk to me."

Mia focused the people coming toward them and listened.

"Right, ten minutes." Jake snapped off the phone. "Anything?"

Ready to shake her head, Mia's eyes widened. She spotted a head covered with a navy hood. It was March and still cold at night. It made sense they could see more than one person wearing a hooded sweatshirt. But seeing more than one navy blue hood was disconcerting. "I think there is someone back there."

Pulling her in front of him, Jake stared in her eyes. "Here's the plan. We head to Macy's front exit. If anything happens and we get separated, head for book store and hide until I find you. Okay?"

Brow wrinkled, Mia nodded. "Why—"

"Let's move." Jake pulled her arm in his and started walking toward the opposite end of the mall.

"We should stay together." Even as the words left her mouth, she regretted them. She could do this on her own. Working with Jake, leaning on his strength, made her second-guess her decision to search for the evidence. He made her feel protected. She couldn't deny she liked having Jake by her side, but wasn't his problem.

"We will," Jake tugged her to a stop. They stood next to a store's three-dimensional glass display window sticking out in the hallway.

Looking past the gorgeous shoes and handbags in the window, Mia saw why Jake had paused. She ignored the displays and stared through the glass. "Can you see anyone?"

"Still back there," Jake grunted. Tightening his grip on her arm, he started walking faster. "This might get tricky, but we don't have a choice."

"What might get—"

"Hey," Jake snapped at a man in a dark cap as he brushed past them, almost knocking Mia down.

She gasped, but at the last second, recognized the man turning away. "Was that—"

"Yeah, keep walking. We have to hurry." Jake's long stride carried them through the glass doors and out on the street in front of the store. "It's a black Corolla, parked beside the sidewalk."

"You can't park there—"

"That's why we need to hurry. We don't want a ticket." Jake lunged toward the right. "There. Run."

Mia's feet were still moving as she grabbed the door handle and pulled it open. Clasping the shopping bag to her chest, she lunged into the seat and slammed the door. "Is he following?"

Jake slammed the driver's door and turned the key in the ignition. "Can't tell, but the good news is that we have a head start."

"Unless he has a partner." Mia twisted in the seat to look back over her shoulder. No one with a hood or a navy shirt appeared in view as Jake steered the car out of the parking lot.

Once back on the highway, the road behind them vacant, he spewed air past his lips. "Check the glove box. Dan left a phone in there."

"It's here. Two of them." Mia sent a glance in his direction. "We're keeping the phone companies in business."

Jake kept one hand on to the wheel and dug his cell phone out of his pocket. "Take the battery out of this, quick. And toss—"

"That's littering."

Turning a disbelieving look in her direction, Jake almost choked on his words. "Two women were murdered, and you're worried about littering?" Mumbling under his breath, he wheeled the car into a gas station. "Give me the battery and the phone."

Leaving the car in neutral, he jumped out. Heel on the battery, he crunched the plastic, and threw it in the wastebasket with the phone.

Mia stared straight ahead as he climbed back in the car and

slammed the door. "I'm just saying—"

"You're right." Jake sent the car speeding back on the highway. "I admire your determination."

🚲

Determination?

Mia toweled her hair dry with fierce swipes. She could think of things she would rather Jake admire other than her determination. *Things like the way she felt in his arms.* Okay. She was out of line. They were trying to solve a murder, not build a relationship.

But she had thought of little else since Jake kissed her at the mall. Even the hours they had spent poring over files from Leigh Anne's computer hadn't distracted her from her reaction to Jake's kiss. She saw Jake was staring at the laptop and frowned. "Do we have to turn the lights off after dark?"

"Dan called the neighbors. Told them he had friends staying a few days, but neighbors aren't the problem." Jake glanced up from the computer. "If anyone staked out this house, lights will give us away."

"No one followed us home. How would they know where we're staying?"

"We don't know when they identified your Honda. I don't think anyone followed us, but I thought we were safe on the way home. I didn't check traffic as close as I should have."

Mia dropped to sofa across from Jake. "Find anything?"

"I'm not sure. You take a look while I get a shower." He passed the computer to Mia on his way down the hall.

She sighed. All these loose ends. They needed evidence. Some connection that proved Phil wasn't involved, but what were they looking for?

Eyes on the screen, her mind wandered to the sound of the shower in the bathroom down the hall. Images of Jake, shedding his clothes and climbing in the shower sent her pulse racing. When this was over, would she ever see him again? Would they ever have a regular conversation? A real dinner? Did he want to? How long could she hide the fact that his glance turned her bones weak?

If they lived though this...

That's what she needed to focus on. Their lives were at risk. Two people had died. She and Jake would add to the total if they didn't find the killer before he found them. No more drooling over thoughts of Jake with a towel wrapped around his waist. This wasn't the time.

Pam Foley's boss, Edward Poole should be her focus. Digging through one file after the other, Mia read a series of e-mails she hadn't noticed before. They were from Edward Poole to Thomas Goldman. E-mail between the four VPs shouldn't cause alert. But Mia noticed the large number of messages between only two of the VPs. Shouldn't all four VPs exchange about the same amount of information?

"I think I found something." Mia said the instant Jake came back in the room. It was a good thing she had spoken before she looked at him, because the sight of Jake with his hair still damp from the shower and his clean-shaven face sent her heart into over-drive.

"Show me." Jake sat down beside her.

Mia did a mental eye roll. How could she focus on facts when the scent of his aftershave filled her head? She couldn't breathe without tasting his scent on her tongue. She wanted to curl into the heat of his body and let the world go by…and then what?

Save the world…save Jake. Save their lives.

"See this list of emails? I highlighted the ones from Poole and Goldman. Look how few are left."

"Mmm," Jake stared at the computer screen. "Looks like you narrowed down the number of suspects. One of these guys hardly gets any mail."

Searching the internet for information about Allan Yow, they ended up with nothing. Mia sighed. "Guess we can rule Alan Yow out."

Jake rubbed his hand across his face, trying to clear his head and block out Mia's image. She was curled against his side so they could both see the computer screen, but her clean scent and the warmth of her body enticed him to forget business and focus on the woman ruining his concentration.

"We should make some calls." He stared at the laptop, waiting for her reaction.

"Who?"

"Edward Poole." Jake watched emotions chase across her face. "You think he's dirty, don't you?"

"He's the one that got Phil involved in all this."

"Then we use that connection as our opening."

Eyes wide, Mia stared at him. "How?"

Staring at the drapes covering the darkness outside the windows, Jake sighed. "Are you willing to bend the truth a little?"

"But you're...a judge."Her lips quivered, giving him the only hint of her deep emotions. The need to taste her lips again added to the longing building in his gut.

"First, I'm a man trying to solve a murder to stay alive. How about it?"

"If it will help us catch a murderer. What do you want me to do?"

"Interview Edward Poole."

Jerking upright, Mia stared at him. "Won't that blow our cover? Assuming he lives to talk to me about it."

"Your name hasn't been mentioned on the news." Jake arched a brow, inviting her to fill in the blanks. If her name hadn't been connected to the murders, they had a free get out of jail card. She could interview their suspects.

"If he won't talk...I'll tell him Phil sent me. He wouldn't dare make a senator start asking questions."

"Arrange the interview, and then throw away the phone."

Mia heard the warning. His caution replayed in her head as she walked to the bedroom. Her hand trembled as she pulled the phone out of her jeans. Could Edward Poole be the killer?

Ten minutes later, Mia clicked off the phone. "He sounds agitated."

"Did he agree to talk to you?"

"Tonight, at eleven at Grover's." She stared down at the phone and frowned, unwilling to voice her unease.

"I don't like it." Jake jumped to his feet. "Grover's will be crowded that time of night."

Keeping her expression blank, Mia said. "He won't have time to plan any tricks if we go now."

Jake lifted the edge of the curtain and stared out the dark window. "It could be a trap."

"He hasn't had time to organize anything."

Jake frowned. "Unless he's behind these murders and he's the one following us." He dropped the curtain back in place and sighed. "It's a risk."

Mia headed back to the bedroom to get dressed. "It's a chance we have to take."

Chapter Eleven

Jake backed Dan's Ford Explorer out of the two-car garage and hit the remote to close the door. "I don't like making all this noise. We don't want to attract attention."

Mia fastened her seatbelt. "It's only ten o'clock. Most houses still have several lights on. The neighbors are probably watching TV."

"Let's go over the plan again."

Staring in the dim light from the dash, Mia tried to see his face. "I'm going to ask Poole how company employees are reacting to the deaths of two co-workers, and try to get him to talk about the women."

"That line of questions only gets you so far. We need to discover connections. Those women were killed for a reason." Jake pushed down the gas. The large vehicle picked up speed as they pulled out of the lakeside community and headed down Hwy 751. "We need to make Poole squirm."

"If he picks up on my mood, that shouldn't be hard." Mia sighed.

"We don't have to do this." Jake glanced at her profile.

"If I can rattle him, maybe he'll give us some hints." Mia bit her lip. "I need to get under Poole's skin."

"Let's talk about what you need to do in Grover's." Jake took his eyes of the road for a second. "How well do you know the place?"

"I've had lunch there several times, and met friends for drinks after work." Mia shrugged.

"Good, you know the layout?"

Mia tried to remember the inside of the remodeled tobacco warehouse. "Two doors into the bar and grill, and one exit from the poolroom in the back, that's all I remember."

"Two exits sound good. There should be a crowd." He focused on the road as they crossed the bridge over backwater from Jordan Lake. "I'll sit at the high table near the bar so I can keep an eye on the room."

Turning toward him, Mia frowned. "Did you wear your disguise?"

"Yep, got my glasses," Jake replied, patting his shirt pocket. "Don't want anyone recognizing me. I'm the only link anyone knows about for now."

⚲

A roar of noise greeted Mia as she walked in the door of Grover's. The bar and grill was crowded and she paused. When they came out of the parking garage adjacent to Grover's patio, they separated and entered by different doors. Where was Jake?

He assured her that a large crowd of people was good, because no one would pay them any attention. Then she spotted him standing at the tall table near the bar as he planned.

Scanning the huge remodeled warehouse, Mia spotted the man she had researched on the internet. Except for his black hair, everything about him looked different. Edward Poole, looked ten years younger in casual workout gear, she noticed when she stopped at his table.

"May I join you?" Mia held her breath.

Poole's sculpted lips curled as his dark eyes roamed over her from head to toe. "You don't look like a reporter."

Hearing the seductive tone in his voice, Mia understood how Pam Foley had fallen for her boss. "I didn't expect to have to leave my bed to get an interview."

"You should have mentioned you were in bed," he purred in a practiced tone.

Back rigid, Mia tilted her chin. "This is business."

"You wanted to talk. What is this about?"

Those melting dark eyes roamed over her, settling on her chest. Mia clenched her fists to keep from cringing. "Your company

121

makes news all the time, Mr. Poole. When two secretaries from one company are murdered, people notice. Questions pop up."

Color slashed his high cheekbones. "Those deaths were unfortunate, but they have nothing to do with Stern-McHamlin."

"How can you be sure? Both women were murdered."

Poole leaned over the table, sending a whiff of expensive cologne floating around Mia. The heavy, musky scent filled her nostrils. For a second, she thought she was going to lose the contents of her stomach on the slick VP.

"My company is dealing with the deaths of two employees. If you want to twist that into something it isn't, that puts your paper on the line. If that's all you want, I'm done."

"Mr. Poole, I'm sorry. I think we got started on the wrong foot. I'm not accusing you or the company of anything. I wanted to find out how your employees are coping with these deaths to give the public a personal angle to the tragedy." Holding her breath in hopes her conciliatory tone had soothed his ruffled feathers, Mia waited.

Looking at her, as she were something stuck to his shoe, Poole leaned back in his seat. "It's been a shock."

Mia sucked in a breath of air and caught the odor of too many bodies crammed into one spot. The mix of smoke, cologne, and alcohol was overpowering. Would she ever forget the stench of smoke?

"How are you handling this personally?" When his head reared back, she held up a placating hand. "I ask only because one of the women was your personal secretary. That must make this situation even more difficult for you than other personnel."

"You're right, of course." Poole brushed a hand over his hair. Mia held back a snort. He hadn't touched a strand of the stylishly arranged hair. "These deaths are personal. Forgive me if grief caused me to over-react."

Like I believe that. Mia stared into his fathomless eyes. "Do police have any leads?"

His eyes darkened as his glare bored into her. "You need to interview the police for those details."

Attempting another angle, Mia said. "I can't imagine how hard it must be, losing a valued secretary and trying to carry on with business at the same time. I'm sure you're as anxious as the family to have this resolved. Are you training a replacement?"

Poole glanced around the room. "We have a large office staff. Finding another secretary isn't the problem."

Crossing her fingers under the table in hopes his ego would make him answer, Mia kept her voice low. "What is the biggest challenge when something like this happens?"

Looking at her from squinted eyes, Poole seemed to decide she wasn't a threat. Shoulders drooping, he switched tactics again as his tone begged for sympathy. "Recovering all the things my secretary knew. Pam Foley was my trusted assistant. Part of her worth was the things she kept in her head to use at a moment's notice."

"You're missing information?" Mia's heart raced. "How will you manage? What will you do?"

Poole's dark eyes flattened like a shark's and he pushed up from the table. "We're done here."

Sensing that she had lost the edge, Mia tried one more comment. "Thanks for the interview, Mr. Poole," she stared up at him, her fingers crossed. "By the way, my brother sends his regards. You remember, Senator Clark?"

Poole turned the color of cottage cheese. His tall slim form swayed over the table for an instant, before he fell back in his seat. "You're Phil Clark's sister?"

As if he didn't know. Mia made a mental snort and nodded her head. He wouldn't be sitting here if he hadn't recognized her name. That told her two things. Edward Poole knew more than he was saying and she couldn't eliminate him as the murderer.

Brow arched, Mia stared at the Teflon-like businessman and tried to hide her distaste. She liked a man who wasn't afraid to get dirty. A man who dug in, up to his elbows when there was a problem. Someone like Jake.

"Didn't you know Phil had links to the press, Mr. Poole? Really, I expected a man in your position to do better research than that."

"What are you implying, Ms. Clark?"

"Not a thing, Mr. Poole." Mia shrugged. "You met my brother, invited him to speak at your club. Knowing he's a politician, I would have expected a man in your position to check him out."

"Ms. Clark. I like plain speaking." Poole twisted his lips in a sneer. "The senator didn't speak to my club, it was a company function. And you're talking in riddles."

Mia wondered what had Pam Foley seen in this man? At first glance, she assumed it was his good looks, but ten minutes of conversation with the man made her feel she needed a bath. How could Pam Foley not know he was a slug?

"Actually, I'm not, Mr. Poole. If you think there's more to this conversation than wanting to find out the mental state of your employees after two tragedies, maybe I should be the one digging deeper for information."

"Calm yourself, Ms. Clark. I'm wound up because a good friend and employee died." Poole's dark eyes made another assessing inventory of Mia's upper body. "You seem very emotional about someone you didn't know, unless…did you know my secretary, Ms. Clark?"

Oh, help. Had she blown her cover? Mia took a slow breath. If he said her name one more time in that slimy tone, she was going to…

"You're right, Mr. Poole. I find the deaths of two local women senseless and upsetting. That's why I called to ask you for an interview." Mia gritted her teeth as his eyes focused on her chest again.

When he glanced up, a satisfied expression covered his smooth face. Lifting a hand, he inspected his manicured nails. The polished surface reflected light. "Yes, it is upsetting."

Deciding she wasn't going to get any more information from him, Mia pushed out of her seat. "Of course, I want to interview other members of your company. I'll let you know when the article is finished, if you like."

Poole's shoulders straightened. "What interviews do you have lined up?"

Noting the tension in his dark glance, Mia forced a fake smile. "You know I can't reveal my sources, Mr. Poole. Thank you for talking to me."

She whirled on her heel and headed toward the door leading to the patio. Had she pushed him too far? Would he cave under her thinly veiled threats and give her a lead?

Pushing through the door, Mia mingled with the customers going to the outside dining area. Even at this time of night, with the chilly March air, several tables were occupied and a crowd surrounded the patio's bar.

Joining the crunch lined up for the bar, Mia kept her eyes on the exit she used. Would Poole follow her? If he came out before she found Jake, they might lose him.

Two minutes later, Poole came out the door and stood, as his dark stare searched the area around the tables.

Mia held her breath, waiting for his black gaze to find her, but the umbrella over the bar and the crowd squashing her against the counter, kept her hidden.

Poole gave one last long look around the crowd, then moved to the edge of the lighted patio and pulled out his cell phone.

Mia couldn't hear what he said, but she watched his body language. Shoulders rigid, he waved a hand in the air as he talked. Then he snapped off the phone and shoved it in the pocket of his workout jacket.

"Could you read his lips?" Jake's breath warmed her cheek as he leaned on the bar beside her.

"No, but he is not happy." She watched as Poole loped down the steps to the parking garage and disappeared among the vehicles. "Should we follow?"

"Can't," Jake shook his head. "He might see you. Get ready to make a run for the SUV as soon as his car pulls out."

Headlights from a car parked on the first row facing the patio, spotlighted the crowd

"Is that him?" Mia twisted around to get a better look at the garage twenty feet away.

"I'm going to the SUV. He won't recognize me. I need to see what he's driving." Jake started away, but turned back to Mia. "Wait until he leaves and stay out of sight."

"I'm going with you. What will it hurt if he sees me?" Mia pushed away from the bar. "He knows I'm here. Just because he didn't see me when he came out doesn't mean I was hiding."

"Good point. I don't like leaving you alone. Stay behind me. Pretend we aren't together, in case he decides to check you out."

"There you go, trying to protect me, again. I'm a reporter, Jake. I can take care of myself."

"When you're with me, keeping you safe is my job." Jake took a couple of long strides, descending the steps in a rush and suddenly, they were as far apart as two strangers.

Mia glanced behind her to check for anyone acting suspicious. Jake's vigilance made her uneasy, but nothing caught her attention. Why was he being so cautious?

She turned back, almost losing sight of Jake in the dim light of the parking garage. A sleek, dark sports car, wheeled out of a space on the opposite side of the garage. Mia was too far away to see the driver, but Jake was close.

Jake stumbled to a stop at the side of the car, and held up his hands, indicating to the driver that he was okay. He waited for the vehicle to pull away, and rushed toward the Ford Explorer.

Mia checked behind her again. When she didn't see anyone following her, she ran to the passenger door. Climbing in as Jake crawled behind the wheel, she gasped. "Was that Poole?"

"Yeah, let's see where he's going." Jake made a couple of quick maneuvers and sent the Explorer shooting out the exit behind the sports car. "If I follow too close, he might notice."

Twenty minutes later, they had trailed the sports car across town to an up-scale housing development. Jake eased the Explorer down the street and parked half a block from where the black car stopped. "What's he doing?"

"This isn't the address I have for Poole, so he isn't going home." Mia stared at the shadowy figure climbing out of the low car. "Mid-night is a strange time to go visiting."

"Unless he has a girlfriend."

"Another one?" Mia kept her eyes on Poole's shadow. "He has a wife and Leigh Anne on the side, according to Pam."

"They're dead. He might have replacements." Jake glanced toward her in the dark. "Do you think this is a crime of passion? Getting rid of the old girlfriends, making way for new ones?"

"I guess not. He's talking to a man." Mia nodded to two shadows merging in front of one of the houses. "Can you tell who it is?"

"Not in this light." Jake hit the steering wheel with his hand. "I'm guessing that was his idea." Five seconds later, another shadowy figure joined them. Jake reached for the ignition key. "Get ready to duck out of sight. We need to see who he's talking to."

Mia unbuckled her seatbelt and strained forward so she could see as the car moved closer. One man's shadow turned in the direction of the noise of their engine, but the other two didn't move.

Blinking to clear her vision, Mia waited.

Jake pulled out, catching three men in the beams of the Explorer's headlights.

Edward Poole had his back to them, giving Mia a clear view of Thomas Goldman and a third shadow. She gasped as she ducked below the dashboard. "It's Alan Yow."

"You're sure?" Jake pressed on the gas and steered out of the residential street.

"I have all their pictures on file. That was Alan Yow." Mia stared at Jake as she straightened up in her seat and fastened her seatbelt. "Why are the VPs meeting this time of night?"

Jake's brow wrinkled. "What did Poole tell you?"

"Nothing," Mia sighed. "I thought he was going to leave the minute I started asking questions."

"I saw him start to get out of the booth. What did you say to rile him?"

Mia shrugged. "I asked how he was adjusting to the tragedy, personally."

Snorting, Jake glanced at her. "You went for the jugular a little early, didn't you?"

"He calmed down when I assured him my interest was only in the emotional reactions of his employees to the deaths of two fellow workers."

"That's all you got?"

Shrugging, Mia sighed. "He went rigid when I mentioned my brother. But I told him I was sure he already knew of the connection since any good businessman investigated his contacts just like reporters did."

"Hell—"

"What? Is someone following us?" Mia struggled to turn in the seat to look at the road behind. "How long has that car been back there?"

"Since we passed those men standing in the dark."

"Why didn't you say—"

"Hang on. I'm going to make a quick turn." Jake glanced back in the mirror. "Good, the light gave us a break."

"Not the mall, again." Mia stared at the road ahead and the entrance to Center Towne Mall parking lot. She choked out the last word and grabbed for the dash as Jake slung the Explorer through the curved entrance. "Who is following us this time?"

"Man, I wish we were in your Honda. This thing isn't made for fast turns." Jake sent the Explorer flying through the parking area. Then, tires screeching, he stopped in an area of the lot dark with shadows. "One of the security lights must be out. Drop down out of sight."

Mia scrambled out of her seatbelt and fell to the floor, clutching a hand against the rapid thumping in her chest. "Can you see anything?"

"Not yet. He's caught in traffic at the light." Jake crouched behind the headrest and twisted to look out the back window. "There, he is…maybe. It's a dark car, going very slow."

"How can you be sure he's following us?" Mia eased up so she could see out the driver's window. "Oh, hurry, get down. He's coming this way."

"Toward us or surveying the lot?" Jake pressed back against the seat.

"He's crawling through the lot, taking his time. We're okay. Look now. He turned to go back the other way. Do you recognize the car?"

"You think it's Yow?" Jake asked as he stared at the taillights of the departing vehicle.

"Don't you?" She eased up get a better view. "It's a sports ca— wait! He's turning back. Get down. Get down."

Jake's glance held hers in the dim light. "You know the risk of playing chicken?" He reached out to grasp her hand. "You can win and still be riddled with bullet holes. I don't want you to get hurt."

"Don't worry about me." Mia tightened her grip on his hand and pulled him over the console.

"Get down as low as you can." Jake leaned over her as she crouched on the floor in front of the seat. "You're special, Mia. I can't believe I'm putting you in danger like this."

Her face pressed to the passenger seat by his weight, Mia said. "Jake, when this is over, I'm going to kiss you."

He chuckled.

She felt his breath vibrate against her head as he leaned over her. "Jake?"

"Yeah?" His whisper echoed hers.

"I couldn't have done this without you. I think I'm in love with you."

Silence echoed so loud inside the Explorer, she heard her heart thump in her chest.

Finally, Jake's breath puffed through her hair. His words were soft as a sigh on the wind when he whispered. "You can't love me. My wife died because of loving me."

Outside, the noise of a car engine sounded loud as a bulldozer as it idled alongside their vehicle.

Mia's breath caught. She grabbed for a hold on Jake, gripping his collar in her fist. His harsh breathing sounded over the thudding of her heart.

The vehicle's engine eased closer. Headlights illuminated their SUV. Just as Mia thought she was taking her last breath, a new noise interrupted the stillness of the night. The crackle of static from a police radio sounded loud over the idle of an engine.

"No!" Mia's breath gushed out in protest. "Not the police. Not now. They'll lock us up."

"Don't move." Jake breathed next to her ear. "Don't make a shadow."

"Police are worse than the slasher—"

"Shhhhh," Jake's arms clutched around her, gripping tight as if he would never let her go. "You'll be okay."

The sound of an engine roared near by, tires squealed and the vehicle raced away.

A voice sounded over the radio static near Jake's door. "Suspicious vehicle headed for the westside lot, over."

A car door slammed. An engine gunned. Lights flickered, and dimmed as the police car turned away. Darkness engulfed the interior of the Explorer.

Mia let out breath she hadn't realized she was holding. "Are they gone?"

Jake eased off her and looked out the car window. "Yeah, nothing's moving. I think you can get up."

"I'm not sure my legs still work." Mia pushed up with her arms and lifted enough to fall in the seat. Her leg muscles cramped, sending pain shooting down to her toes. "Good thing we didn't have to run. My feet have gone to sleep."

Jake chuckled as he stared around the dark lot. "We should be safe to move now."

"Wait, with all those police cars out there, maybe we should stay put."

Darkness wrapped around them. Feeling almost safe after the scare of headlights aimed at their windows. Mia gulped a breath and released it on a long sigh. She heard Jake inhale a deep breath and bit her lip. "Jake…about what I said—"

"Danger makes people say strange things. We're safe, now." Jake stared out the side window, keeping his head turned away from her.

Did he regret the comment about his wife? Hands clenching into fists, Mia had the sudden urge to hit out at something, or someone. "Let's go."

🚲

"What do we know about Alan Yow?" Jake demanded as they entered the house after a near silent ride home following their incident.

Neither of them mentioned the tense moments they had thought were their last. Bullets could have riddled their bodies and they would have been helpless. And neither mentioned the words they had uttered.

Jake didn't regret telling Mia she was an amazing woman. That realization had slipped up on him, but the longer they were together, the more he knew it was true. It wasn't just the way she made him want to grab hold of life, it was her determination, and her focus on doing what she thought was right.

He could see parts of him and his wife in Mia's dedication. For the first time since a drunk driver had collided with his wife's car and left her and his three-year-old son dead, Jake wanted to embrace all life offered.

The threat of being so close to Mia, and having to watch her die, of feeling the life drain out of her because of bullet holes in her body, had brought the pain of his wife's death back. In the instant those car lights blared in their windows, the stalker's vehicle competing with the roar of his heart, Jake realized he was ready to fight to live, to protect Mia.

He had reached for the gun tucked in his waistband, ready to shot to save Mia's life. He hadn't been able to save his wife and child. The fact that he hadn't been in the car to die with them had weighed heavy on his conscience for the past six years.

His brain understood he couldn't go back, and finally, tonight in that mall parking lot, his heart accepted that fact as well. He had made the choice to move on and face the future when he pulled out his gun. Now, he had to deal with the realization that he wanted his future to include Mia.

Fighting the urge to rush over to Mia and hold her in his arms to prove she was safe took all his strength. Shrugging out of his jacket, he watched as she opened up the laptop. "Do you want coffee?"

Not glancing up, Mia shook her head. "I'm wired enough without adding caffeine. I need to check these files."

Chewing on her lip, Mia forced her gaze to the screen as the laptop booted up. Had she really said those words? In those last seconds when she was certain they would die, had she really told Jake she loved him?

How had that happened?

She never exposed her emotions to a man...and now she was wondering why. Why Jake? Family was everything to her, always had been, even when she was a little girl. She had loved her father's attention, and longed to get close to her mother.

That longing had put her in this situation. But since her father's death, she had missed the unconditional love she lost when he died. Looking back at her relationships, she missed the feeling that she meant something special to another person. Until now. Until she met Jake.

Inhaling a quivering breath, she blinked moisture from her eyes and stared at the screen. The file on Alan Yow wasn't very large. Compared to the other VPs, he was low key and kept out of the news.

Had she really told Jake she loved him?

Clearing her throat, she risked a glance as Jake lounged in the stuffed chair across from her. But his thoughtful expression sent heat spiraling to her mid-section. He hadn't responded when she'd said she loved him. A gut wrenching fear of rejection curled in her stomach. Why had she said those words and embarrassed them both? Why tell a man she loved him because she thought she was going to die? *Why not run?*

Because she couldn't get out of the car, that's why. Even if she had managed to get the door open and crawl out, she wouldn't have left Jake alone and in danger. Shocking as it was to her numb brain, she had been ready to die with Jake.

It was an amazing discovery, but true. That put Jake right up there with her mother and brother as people she would protect with her last breath.

She loved him!

"Could we save this until morning? My brain is half-asleep." She pushed back against the sofa as she glanced at Jake. There were dark circles under his eyes from lack of sleep, but he looked strong and ready to take on the world.

"Yeah, sure. We need to get some sleep." His gaze rested on her for several seconds. "I'll look over the files and then hit the sack."

Jake whistled tunelessly as he watched Mia walk out of the room. Where did they go from here? What could he say to get them back to normal? Did he want to go back?

Ignoring his feelings for Mia meant returning to the gray life he had endured for the past six years. Mia added color and excitement to his existence. Was he over reacting to the danger of their evening? When this was over, would he feel this need to protect her? It was time he faced the possibility that the tension between them was real.

He had to stop protecting his heart. Six years was long enough to live in a vacuum. It was time he faced the future and took his chances. His heart deserved the chance to love, again.

Chapter Twelve

Charles Herne," Mia announces as she rushed into the kitchen the next morning.

"Leigh Anne Saddler's boss," Jake said at the same time.

Mia managed a smile as she took the cup of coffee he offered. "We're on the same page, it seems."

Shrugging, he sipped the hot brew. "Tell me what you know about Herne while I whip up some eggs."

Going to the den for the laptop, Mia settled on a stool at the breakfast bar. "Why wasn't he meeting with the other men last night?"

Jake looked up from cracking eggs in a bowl. "Did he date either of the women?"

"He is VP of product development and he dated his secretary, Leigh Anne Saddler." Mia read the files. "That's it. We have nothing."

Jake turned fluffy scrambled eggs on two plates and added toast. "Sounds like you need to give Herne a call."

"Another interview?" Mia asked around a forkful of eggs. "Um, these are delicious. Where did you learn to cook?"

"My wife. Sara was a home economics teacher and she insisted I learn to take care of myself."

Shivering at his words, Mia forced a chuckle. "Smart woman."

"Yeah, she was a good mother, too." Jake stabbed at the toast with his fork.

Mia's breath caught. "You had a child?"

Nodding, Jake met her glance. "A son. He turned three a week before the accident."

Perched on stools, they were sitting so close their elbows almost touched, but Mia felt as if the Grand Canyon had appeared between them. There was so much she didn't know about Jake, and yet, she loved him.

"I'm so sorry." Tears clogged the back of her throat. "How did you survive a tragedy like that?"

Shoulders hunched, Jake raked the fork across the empty plate. "I retreated in my shell and watched life go by."

"D-do you want to talk about it?"

Long seconds passed. "His name was Steven. He had Sara's blonde hair and my eyes, and a laugh we couldn't resist." Jake swiped at his eyes. Shaking his head, he sighed. "Stevie was a little dare devil. Always into something. Losing them left a hole in my life that can never be filled."

"He sounds perfect." Mia blinked furiously. "I don't know how you managed."

"One day at a time until you barged into my life." Jake stared in her eyes. "That thing you said…about loving me. I liked that. Being with you, helping you has brought new meaning to my life. I owe you for that."

Heart thumping, Mia held his gaze. "I don't want you to owe me, Jake. I want—"

His lips settled on hers smothering her words. His lips were warm and tasted of coffee. Mia wiggled closer and wrapped her arms around his shoulders.

Every nerve in her body snapped to alert. Jake made her feel in ways she had never known possible. He said she'd brought him back to life, but he showed her what life meant, and she wanted more. When he broke the kiss, she couldn't hold back a moan.

He leaned in and kissed her again, not a sweet lingering kiss like the first, but a hot demanding kiss that left her breathless when he broke away.

Tracing a finger along her cheek, he sighed, then stood up and gathered their plates. "Business first. Call Herne. Set up a meeting."

⚘

Grover's was buzzing with noise from the lunch crowd when they arrived to meet with Charles Herne. They followed the same plan, entered by separate doors, and Jake found a seat at the tall bar table facing the booths so he could keep an eye on Mia. Not difficult as she was sitting about twenty feet away.

His gut twisted as he eyed the blond haired man sitting across from her. Kissing her had been a mistake. Teeth grinding, he stirred the lemon slush he ordered, and acknowledged the truth. He shouldn't have kissed her. Even three hours later, he could feel her lips under his and her scent filled his head.

Watching as she put herself in danger by meeting Herne went against his need to protect her. He hadn't been able to save his wife, but finally, he accepted that he wasn't responsible for her death.

He had to back off and give Mia space. She was flirting with danger, but this was her fight. She needed to clear her brother's name to ease her conscience, and all he could do was watch, because Jake knew how heavy guilt could weigh on a person's conscience.

Twirling the glass in his hands, his thoughts returned to the morning news report. Police were still looking for two killers, and that worried him. From TV reports, cops hadn't connected the two women's murders, other than the fact that both women worked for the same company.

After reading Mia's files, and experiencing their own skirmishes with danger, his gut told him the cops were missing something. But what? He needed evidence to show them, and he needed it fast. One more encounter like the one last night in the mall parking lot, might be their last.

Mall security had almost discovered them hiding in the Explorer, but what worried him more was the sports car that followed them. Did Charles Herne drive a sports car? There was no way Edward Poole could have reached his car in time to follow them...was there?

🚲

"Thanks for meeting me, Mr. Herne." Mia smiled at the attractive blond haired man across the table.

"Call me Charles," he smiled a toothpaste commercial smile, "Edward said you might call. I hope you don't mind meeting at the same place you met him. This is convenient to the office."

Convenient to set up a trap, too. Mia fought the urge to look for Jake and kept her eyes on Charles Herne. "Grover's is great. I love the food here."

"You didn't ask to meet with me to talk about food, did you?"

Lifting a shoulder, Mia met his questioning gaze. "I wanted to get your reaction to the recent deaths of your company employees."

Herne's expression tightened to a mask. "Of course, you know Leigh Anne Saddler was my secretary."

"That's why I wanted an interview."

"Sad. So senseless." Herne's smooth brow wrinkled. "Leigh Anne wouldn't hurt a flea. One look at her lush body and people thought she was a bimbo, but she was smart." He stared at his drink as if he'd never seen it before. "I miss her."

"What bout Pam Foley, did you work with her?" Mia watched for any sign that Herne was stringing her along, but saw none.

Herne shrugged with a nonchalance fitting for his high powered position in the company, but missing until now. "The usual, I would see her at meetings in the conference room and speak to her around the office. Truthfully, I didn't know her very well. But her death is a waste, just the same." Fists clenched on the table in front of him, he stared at Mia. "Why kill these women? Why murder women who were contributing to society?"

"I'm sorry for your loss—"

"Yeah, me, too." Charles Herne stared at Mia from eyes bright as a spring sky and glistening like drops of rain. "You know I dated Leigh Anne?"

Mia swallowed, surprised by his candor. "W-was it serious?"

Herne blew out a sigh. "It was for me." He leaned forward. "I realize this admission gives me motive, but I cared about Leigh Anne, even after she called things off."

"I'm sorry." Mia crossed her fingers under the table. "When did she break things off with you?"

"Are you asking how long did I have to plan her murder?" Herne shook his head and sighed. "I didn't kill her." Voice low, he stared in Mia's eyes. "I loved her."

"What happened?" Mia felt a pang of sorrow for his obvious distress. "Was it another man?"

Herne's eyes glazed over as if he was remembering the past. "Yeah, one of the other company VP's." He held up a hand, "She didn't flaunt it in my face if that's what you're thinking."

"I'm not—"

"I am a jealous ex-lover." Herne said as he blew a gusty sigh. "Look at me. I turn fifty this year. My youth is behind me, but not my dreams. Leigh Anne stole my heart and gave me hopes for a future with someone I could spend the rest of my life with, then she dumped me."

"You know—"

"I'm providing a motive for killing her?" Herne shook his head. "Yeah, but I couldn't hurt her, even after she started dating another man at the office."

"Edward Poole?" Mia held her breath.

Herne snorted. "That fancy pants? No, their fling was over before I asked Leigh Anne out. Poole was her getting acquainted fling, if you know what I mean."

Mia frowned, "Who was she dating and breaking up with you?"

"The man I would kill, if I were a violent person. Believe me, that *sonofabitch*, Thomas Goldman deserves to die."

Emotions darkened his eyes. His tone, the way he said Leigh Anne's name, everything about him pointed to his love for ex-model. Why had Leigh Anne turned him away for another man? Why date a man in the same office? "How long had she been dating Goldman?"

Herne's shoulders slumped. "I don't know. It was hush-hush. No one in the office knew."

"How did you find out?"

A sheepish look added color to his face. "Have you ever loved one person so much you felt as if they were a part of you, the missing piece in your life? That's how I felt about Leigh Anne."

Mia's breath hitched. Her heart thumped. She recalled her response to Jake's kiss. Charles Herne had just described her feelings for Jake. "I-yes, I know that feeling."

"Then you understand when I say I could read her mind. I knew when Leigh Anne was interested in another man. I knew it was Thomas Goldman."

Mia held his gaze for long seconds. She liked him. The poor man was devastated by Leigh Anne's death. Could her instincts be wrong? Could Charles Herne's emotional words be an act? Had she allowed his blonde haired, blue-eyed, boyish good looks to lead her astray? Was he lying? After one last look in his tortured eyes, she pushed out of the booth. "Thank you for meeting me, Mr. Herne. I am sorry for your loss."

Charles Herne reached out and took her hand. "Promise me you'll find her killer."

Frowning, Mia glanced around to see in anyone had overheard his comment. "I'm a reporter, Mr. Herne, not police detective."

Herne leaned close. "You're looking for more than a human interest story. All the vice presidents are suspicious. How do you think I heard about you? If a reporter's snooping has them this riled up, there must be a reason. Find the truth for me. For Leigh Anne."

For long seconds, Mia held his gaze. Then, giving a nod, she turned to the patio exit. Out of the corner of her eye, she caught a glimpse of Jake at the bar. Would he think she was crazy to trust Herne? What if this was a ploy to throw her off track?

At the exit, Mia glanced over her shoulder at the booth where she had left Herne. He sat staring down at his drink, lost in his grief. Mia pushed against the door handle and stepped out on the patio. Before she could turn to look at the outdoor diners, someone stepped close to her. An arm wrapped her in a tight hug that slammed her face against a hard muscled chest. The assailant's fleece jacket covered her head, leaving her blind and struggling to breath.

Realizing only her legs were all that was visible, Mia struggled against the grip trapping her in a vice. Had Jake used a different exit and beat her to the patio? Was this his attempt to hide her from police? She inhaled, unsure whether to scream or not, and caught a male scent that definitely was not Jake's aftershave.

Panic exploded in her head.

She twisted and shoved, but the bone-crunching grip tightened. A hard chin crushed down on top of her head with enough force and pain to keep her from twisting free. And all during the struggle, the man holding her captive moved steadily toward the entrance to the parking garage right off the patio.

Realizing she was in very serious trouble, Mia tried to scream.

The crushing grip tightened and cut air from her lungs as if the assailant could read her intentions. To prevent her from gaining her footing, the abductor half carried, half dragged her toward the stairs. The brutal grip and the fleece trapped her.

Jake wouldn't spot her because of the sweat jacket over her head. He would see what appeared to be an entwined couple and search elsewhere for her.

If she was going to get away from her abductor, she had to do it herself. She tried to push away, but her captor's grip tightened. Her fear escalated to a new level.

Was the man holding her the killer?

Her assailant didn't smell rank or putrid as she imagined a killer would. His aftershave smelled expensive. His clothes smelled clean. As she twisted in his grip, she caught a glance of his shoes. His white athletic shoes were so spotless they almost glowed.

Who was this man? Was he the slasher? One of the vice-presidents?

Images of the Leigh Anne's slashed throat filled her head. New fears caused her to fight against the binding grip. She would have bruises tomorrow. If she lived that long.

That thought renewed her energy. She couldn't die. She refused to let this man rob her of life as he had Leigh Anne Saddler and Pam Foley.

His attempts to silence her made her more determined to reveal the killer. She'd had a warning, the other two women hadn't. She would not become another victim.

But she was running out of time to escape.

Gouging her fingers furiously into his side, she twisted to loosen his grip, and caught a glimpse of the shallow steps leading to the parking garage. Once they were out of sight of the patio, her assailant could knock her over the head, stow her in the trunk of his car, and no one would realize she was in trouble.

"Mia!"

Jake's shout rang in her ears and called her back to sanity. He couldn't be more than ten feet away, and worried enough to blow their cover by calling her name. Mia increased her struggle to get free of the man holding her. She couldn't leave Jake. Not now. She had just found him. The past few days had taught her more about love than she had learned in a lifetime. She could not lose Jake now.

"Mia! Where are you?"

If Jake's voice could melt her insides, what could his love do? She would never know if she didn't get away from the madman hauling her away. Renewing her efforts to escape, she clawed her nails into the man's back and heard him grunt. The pressure on top of her head eased, but the ache down her neck and back continued.

But pain was good. Pain meant she was alive. For now.

Another twist of her upper body gave her enough freedom from the assailant's grip to lean over and plant her feet on the ground. And not a second too soon.

Steps to the garage were only a yard away.

Ignoring the urge to scream for Jake, she put every ounce of strength she had left into a jab of her right fist and aimed for the assailant's crotch.

He let out a howl of pain and lunged forward, dropping his hold on her as he clamped both hands to his crotch.

Mia stumbled. The man's forward momentum, and the jacket wrapped around her upper body, pulled her to her knees. Her hands hit the brick surface of the patio with enough force to jar her teeth. Fearing a renewed attack, she went rigid. Did the assailant have a knife? Would he slash her throat right here in a public place?

Inhaling on a sob, she shoved backward crab-like, hoping to escape any slash of his blade, and caught her first sight of his hooded shape. Bent double, and still clutching his crotch, the man scrambled down the steps and disappeared in the parking garage.

Relief drained the tension out of her limbs, and she fell on her butt with a thump. Mia sat staring at the spot where the man disappeared and gulped air. She was alive. She was bruised and scared half out of her wits, but she was unharmed. How had she escaped? If this was the slasher, how...

"Mia? Are you okay?" Kneeling beside her, Jake leaned to stare in her face. "Are you hurt? Can you stand?" Taking her hand, he gently pulled her upright. "What happened?"

Pointing to the garage with a shaking finger, she managed to say between gasps for air. "A man grabbed me under his sweat jacket and tried to take me away."

Her words ended in a whisper. Tears rolled down her cheeks. She turned into Jake's embrace and burrowed her head against his chest.

Two minutes earlier, she had been in a similar position with her abductor, but this was different. Jake's warmth felt safe, not threatening. He smelled different. Clean like the attacker, but without the heavy scent of expensive cologne.

Alarms went off in her head. She wanted to stay wrapped in the safety of Jake's arms, but she was convinced she had come into personal contact with the killer. Every nerve in her body went on alert warning her it was true.

"It was him." Mia pushed back enough to see Jake's face. "I know it was him."

"Did you recognize him?"

Sighing with frustration, she shook her head. "He wrapped his sweat jacket around me before I had a chance to see his face, but it was the killer. I know it was."

Jake stared around the parking garage. "He's probably gone by now. He had a head start."

"I hit him in the crotch, so he wasn't moving too fast." Her body quivered, remembering the last few moments in the man's grip.

"Come on, let's have a look. I'm not leaving you alone."

Mia pulled back, a wave of emotions flashed through her head making her feet cling to the pavement. The parking garage was shadowy in broad daylight. After this attempt on her life, she didn't have the energy to fight against her fear of the dark and the attacker.

"I can describe him. A navy sweat jacket, tobacco brown cargo pants and new white athletic shoes."

Jake gently brushed a strand of hair behind her ear. "How do you know the shoes were new?"

"They didn't have a smudge on them until I stomped on his feet, trying to get away."

Jake stared back at the garage.

Mia could feel his tension radiating from his hold on her arms and in the rigid set of his shoulders. Muscles along his jaw rippled like a dragon's back. Jake wanted to chase after her attacker, but he wouldn't leave her.

She understood his urge to give chase, but her encounter with the bad guy had been too close, too frightening. She wanted Jake's comfort. She needed to know he was there, protecting her while she recharged her energy.

With another glance at the garage, Jake gave a slow nod of his head. Wrapping his arm around her shoulders, he pulled her close to his side.

She melted into his warmth and strength. She was safe with Jake. She didn't question that fact, she just knew Jake wouldn't let anything happen to her.

If she had been alert when she walked out the patio door, the assailant wouldn't have grabbed her. If she had waited for Jake, before making her exit, nothing would have happened. But she'd been focused on Charles Herne's comments. Shivering, she snuggled closer to Jake's side. His arm tightened. She sighed. His chin touched the top of her head. She winced and pulled away.

"What's wrong?" Jake frowned.

Running her fingers through her hair, she found the tender spot. "He held my head down with his chin. It's a little sore, but I'm okay."

"Let me look." Jake parted the strands of hair and examined her scalp. "No bleeding, but I see a goose egg."

Mia sighed. "If that's my only injury, I'm lucky."

Jake stared in her eyes for long seconds, then dropped a quick kiss on her lips. "I think it's time to call the police."

Chapter Thirteen

Are you sure? I don't want to be arrested."

Holding up his hand, Jake punched a number in the disposable phone.

"Chief? It's Jake. Any news on the body I found in the courthouse?" Brow furrowed, he listened to the voice on the phone.

Mia studied his strong, handsome face, and then rested her cheek against his chest.

"Chicf, I can't come in. I'm one step away from a murderer." His free hand clenched her waist. Mia could feel the tension in his body as the arm across her back turned to iron.

"I am not a suspect. I don't care what the SBI told you. You know me, Chief. Doesn't being a judge mean anything?"

Mia wiggled so close their bodies made contact from shoulder to knees. Her mind drifted to a different topic, a place with naked bodies and earth shattering kisses, until his words made her dreams disintegrate like a shattered vase.

"I can't be your main suspect, Chief. Someone is trying to kill me. I'm hiding to stay alive, not to avoid the law. You can tell the SBI that the killer tried to abduct my friend less than ten minutes ago."

Mia shuddered. *Friend.* Was that all she was? A friend? How could he sound so aloof? Pushing out of his arms, Mia willed herself to calm down, but the urge to cry almost over-whelmed her.

"I'm not coming in until you catch this guy. He's wearing a navy sweat jacket with a hood, mud brown pants and new white tennis shoes." Jake paused. "Yeah, Chief. I hear you, but I value my life. Catch the killer. He was at Grover's ten minutes ago." Jake clicked off the phone. "We have about a five minute head start. Let's get out of here."

🚲

Fifteen minutes later, sitting in Starbucks cradling a tall iced coffee, Jake stared across the table at Mia. "Hope you don't mind the break. I thought it was a good idea to stay off the road after I called the Chief."

"You didn't throw away your phone."

Jake studied her colorless cheeks, wanting to wring the attacker's neck. Worse, he wanted to shake the Chief and his SBI buddies until their teeth rattled for adding to Mia's worries. "I'll give them a few minutes to trace the call, so they'll know we really were at Grover's."

Brow wrinkled, Mia stared over the tall iced coffee cup with wide blue eyes. "Why?"

"If the chief checks, he'll know I was telling the truth about being in Durham."

"He can trace us here. Is that what you want?" Mia's color turned ghostly. "I can't get arrested, Jake. I've done all this to avoid any brush with the law."

"You risked your life to save your brother. Why?" Jake held up a hand. "And don't give me that line about clearing the senator of false claims. I get that. It sounds crazy, but I'll take your word for it. But you nearly died a few minutes ago and I want to hear the real reason this is so important to you."

"I'm not a good sister." Mia whispered as she stared at passing traffic. "Shouldn't we hide so we can't be seen?"

"Hiding in plain view is safer." Jake lifted a brow. "You were saying?"

Squaring her shoulders, she sighed. "There's always been competition between us."

"And that's bad?" Jake allowed his disbelief to show. "It's obvious you love him, or you wouldn't have risked your life."

"I should have supported him when he went into politics, but I didn't trust his decisions."

Jake settled back in his chair. "It couldn't have been easy, knowing your life was under a microscope because of his choices."

"Things were tense between us before he made that choice. I realize now, I reacted immaturely, but in my heart I know I've always loved him."

"In other words, you have doubts." Jake released a loud breath.

"Wouldn't you? An ex-model claimed she was pregnant with his child. What was I supposed to believe? That he isn't as susceptible to beauty and sex? For one thing, he's a man. Even worse, he's a politician and exposed to temptation at every turn."

"You went to all this risk, doubting your brother's innocence?" Jake shook his head. "That makes no sense."

"Would you believe me if I said my mother made me do it?"

Jake met her gaze. "She couldn't force you. You're an adult."

"I did it because I felt guilty." Mia slammed her cup on the table. "There, are you happy, now?"

Lifting his cup, Jake returned her glare. "It's time to talk to your brother."

Mia shook her head. "He doesn't know about any of this, and I can't tell him. He never makes a move without telling his aides. Details might leak to the media."

"You're a reporter. What's wrong with seeing your name in the news?" Jake leaned close to catch her response.

"My boss goes rabid when a reporter's name appears in the news." Mia shrugged. "I don't want to lose my job. I can't. It's all I have."

Jake held her gaze knowing there was more to the story than she was telling. But finally, he shook his head and said. "You need to find out what your brother knows."

🚲

Ten minutes later, Mia called Phil on her disposable phone. "It's me, how are you?"

"Where the hell are you? Have you read the papers? Your employers are ruining me." Phil's voice roared through the speaker.

Her insides still quivering from the near abduction, Mia put all her energy into keeping her tone civil. "I'm fine, thanks for asking."

"What's wrong? Why wouldn't you be okay? And why can't you stop your editor from printing this trash?"

"So the model is dead?" Mia said.

"Ex-model and you know she is. Your paper printed the story. Are you calling to gloat, Mia? I'm to busy to play childish games."

Mia blew air past her lips and managed a civil tone. "Phil, we need to talk."

"We are talking now and you're wasting my time."

Mia's last hope evaporated. "It's true, isn't it? Everything Leigh Anne Saddler said was true."

"I'm hanging up, now."

"I saw her body," Mia whispered, clenching her fingers around the phone to hold back images of the model's body.

Phil remained silent. She heard the rustle of papers shuffling. Then Phil cleared his throat and demanded in a dead sounding voice. "Why are you calling?"

"Someone just tried to kill me for a second time."

"When? How?"

Mia tightened her grip on the phone. "We need to talk. No staff. No cameras. No recorders. Just us. Okay?"

"I can't just waltz out of the office like a normal person. I'm in the middle of organizing my re-election campaign."

Resisting a very strong urge to stomp on the phone, Mia lost the last restraints on her patience. "If you didn't kill that model, meet me. Convince me."

🚲

"Why did you want to meet outside a church in plain sight, are you crazy. Why all the theatrics?" Phil demanded an hour later when he sat on the bench beside Mia.

Mia glanced at the thick growth concealing several benches along meandering walkways alongside University Methodist Church.

"Hello to you, too, brother dear." She cut a glance in Phil's direction, hardly recognizing him in jeans and a windbreaker. "Are you sure you weren't followed?"

Glaring his displeasure, Phil snapped. "You called Mom?"

"I told her everything was okay. That's all she needs to know."

"You think everything is okay? Are you out of your tiny little mind?" Phil slammed his hand against the wood bench. "What's going on, Mia? What did you mean by saying I need to convince you I'm not a killer. Is this some immature prank with you threatening to go to the cops if I don't play by your rules? Tell me this, why would I kill Leigh Anne?"

"Oh, I don't know." Her teeth grinding, Mia leveled a glare at him. "Maybe because she was pregnant? This is your mess, Phil. Why did you lie about dating Leigh Anne Saddler?"

His mouth opening and closing, Phil sent her a look out of the corner of his eye. "I wouldn't call our arrangement dating. How much do you know?"

"Not enough to stay alive unless we catch the killer." Mia lowered her voice. "In the past three days, I've been locked in a burning building, chased through the woods, followed by more than one car, and just now, someone tried to kidnap me at lunch. I want the truth."

"You can't handle the truth." Phil jumped to his feet and paced in front of the bench. "You were always Dad's golden girl. Always the perfect child. You don't know squat about real life."

"Sit down so you can't be seen from the street." Mia stuffed her hands in her jacket pockets and lifted her face for the cool March breeze to ease the heat racing through her veins. "Mom insisted I do whatever it takes to clear your name. I've done that, Phil." She blew out a sigh. "I breached security to search the courthouse for evidence and almost died for my efforts. I stumbled over the model's body. I can't prove you're innocent if you don't tell me the truth."

"So you can wipe my face in my bad judgment? Finally convince Mom you are the good child?" Phil slouched. After long minutes, he whispered, "Sorry, sis. But the truth isn't that simple."

"I'm not accusing you of anything, or trying to show you up. You're my brother. I love you. But I don't want to die because of a lie."

Sitting up straight, obviously back in control of his emotions, Phil stared at her. "Things are really that dangerous?"

"Two women are dead. What do you think?"

"Oh, God. I never expected this." Phil scraped a hand across his face and stared at his feet. "I appreciate your help. I know it doesn't sound like it, but I really do. I don't want you to get hurt, sis. It's just...I can't face losing everything because of one mistake."

Thinking of Pam Foley, Mia arched her brows. "One?"

Face flushed, Phil turned a shocked stare on her. "How did you find out?"

"Pam Foley told me…about ten minutes before someone killed her."

"You think—"

"All this is connected to you? Yes." Mia touched his shoulder. "Tell me what's going on, before we both end up dead."

"I ruined everything." Phil whispered, staring at his hands. "I have to tell Ellen, don't I?"

"She deserves the truth so she can protect herself and the kids." Mia pulled her hand away from his shoulder.

"Oh, God. I might lose my wife and kids. Why have I been so stupid?"

"If you didn't kill Leigh Anne, who did?" Mia kept her voice firm.

"You can't think I'm a murderer?" Phil's face lost color.

"I know you didn't kill those women, but you need to help me find out who did." Mia curbed her impatience. "What are you involved in, Phil? Why is it worth murdering someone for?"

"From the moment Edward Poole introduced me to Leigh Anne, I couldn't resist her," Phil sighed. "It makes me sound weak, but that's what happened. She turned those hot blue eyes on me and wiggled that lush body and I forgot everything."

Nausea churned in Mia's stomach. "You got her pregnant?"

"No!" Phil cringed as if sex or pregnancy was beneath him. "I could have, but I was careful. We haven't been together for months. Two at least."

"It could still be your child." The words seared Mia's tongue. Her niece or nephew might have been murdered along with their mother. "We haven't heard the coroner's report but she wasn't far enough along to show."

"It wasn't mine. I tell you, it couldn't have been."

Mia tried not to gag. "What about Pam Foley?"

Cheeks red, Phil snapped. "Now that really was stupid."

Mia bit down on her lip to keep from agreeing.

Finally, Phil sighed. "Pam was a nice, not sexy like Leigh Anne. Pam was the kind of woman you take home to meet the parents." He shrugged. "That's what got me in trouble. With Leigh Anne things burned hot and then wham it was over. But Stern-McHamlin kept calling, wanting me to vote in their favor. Pam just showed up one evening, said they sent her to explain company policy."

"It wasn't true?"

"Why are you asking my opinion? I screwed up so many things lately. I don't know what I believe, anymore." Phil huffed. "Do you think Ellen will leave me?"

"I don't know. What you've done...cheating on your wife and betraying her trust, hurts on so many different levels. Pain. Disappointment. Pride. Heartbreak. I don't know what she'll do."

"All I had to do was vote like the company wanted me to and none of this would have happened."

"What's the big deal about the vote?" Mia kept an eye on the streets as Phil filled her in on the depth of Stern-McHamlin's involvement. When he finished, she stared at him as if she were looking at a stranger. Maybe she was. "This all boils down to money?"

"Millions," Phil agreed, with a nod.

"Enough to commit murder for?"

🚲

Mia sighed as she watched Phil mingle with people on the sidewalk outside the church. In the floppy fishing hat and windbreaker, he looked more like a man off to the library than a senator, up for re-election.

If half of what he suspected was true, he wouldn't be a senator long, but he wouldn't be in jail for murder, either.

"Have police questioned him?"

Mia jerked upright as the low voice came from the bushes behind her. Jake was sitting on the other side of the thick row shrubs and azaleas, keeping watch. They had selected this bench for two reasons. Mia could keep an eye on street and Jake could listen to her conversation with Phil and make certain no one else heard.

"Yes." Mia sighed.

Jake walked around the shrubs and sat beside her. "We need to talk to Thomas Goldman."

"It's almost dark." Eyes wide, Mia shivered as she glanced around. "I'd rather meet him in daylight."

"What makes you think he's the killer?" Jake studied the lines of tension marking her face. She looked tired. She hadn't stopped since this event started. A few hours here and there to rest or do research, and then she was back to tracking the killer.

Did Phil Clark know how lucky he was to have Mia for a sister? "After looking at your files, I'd say Thomas Goldman is the top candidate for CEO."

Head tilted, her brow arched. "So he had the most to lose."

"Call him."

Chapter Fourteen

L ater that evening when they arrived at the popular hang out, *He Just Left*, there were so many people, they decided it was safe to enter the patio section of the bar together.

"We're in disguise." Jake insisted, urging Mia forward. "We should be safe."

With the glasses on and his gelled hair combed back from his face, Jake didn't look anything like the firefighter she'd first met. And wearing the blonde wig, she looked different as well. "I hope we don't miss him in this crowd."

"Keep your eyes open."

She watched the line of customers move slowly toward the outdoor bar. "I told him to meet me outside. But maybe we should check upstairs?"

"Nope." Jake nudged her forward. "A man in his position follows orders. I don't want you trapped inside. Keep watching. He'll be here."

Drink in hand, Mia worked her way through the crowd, aiming for the maple tree in the side yard. Laughter and music floated over patrons standing elbow to elbow. She shivered in the chilly evening air. "Do you see a green jacket?"

"Relax. We're in the heart of UNC territory." Jake nodded to the blue and white Tar Heel flags flying from the fence supports. "A green jacket will stand out a mile."

"I'll be glad when this is over." Mia glanced around the crowd and gasped. Her blood turned to ice in her veins as she sputtered. "What's he doing here?"

Alerted by the tension her voice, Jake went rigid. "Who?"

"Alan Yow just came through the gate."

"Is he alone?" Jake tried to check the man out without looking obvious.

"In this crowd, I can't tell." Mia stood on tiptoe to get a better view of the vice president.

"Ignore him. If he feels you staring at him he might get antsy."

Ten minutes later, her heart thudding hard, Mia watched as man in a green jacket joined Alan Yow at the patio bar.

"They're together now," Jake confirmed, lifting his glass.

"Here he comes." Mia said into her glass as she lifted the drink to hide her mouth. "He's alone."

"I lost sight of Yow." Jake mumbled as he turned away so they wouldn't appear to be together if the man in green noticed him. "Don't approach Goldman. Wait until we see what Yow is doing."

"Goldman's just standing there, looking around." Mia said behind the cover of her glass. "He's in plain sight and I don't like waiting."

"This could be a trap." Jake checked the crowd but didn't see any sign of Yow. "How do you want to handle this?"

"I'm going to talk to him." Mia turned away and eased through the groups of chatting patrons. Finally stopping when she was in front of Thomas Goldman. "Is this the green jacket you mentioned?"

Surprise glowed from the icy blue eyes in his handsome face. His perfectly groomed brown hair and elegant white shirt and tie made the vice-president look out of place in this crowd. Most of the people gathered at *He Just Left* wore sweat jackets or chunky collegiate sweaters. Holding her breath, Mia waited for Thomas Goldman to respond.

"They told me you were a brunette." His words were sharp as ice cycles as his frosty gaze roamed over her blonde wig. "Why the disguise?"

"Thanks for meeting me." Ignoring his question, Mia made an attempt to take control of the conversation. "I wanted to ask you some about—"

"If you're here to ask about Leigh Anne Saddler, forget it."

Goldman snapped.

"Is the topic of Pam Foley off limits, as well?" Mia lifted her chin. "Stern-McHamlin lost two employees to tragedy. I wanted to ask how your staff reacted to the shock."

"You expect me to believe that's all you want, Ms. Clark? You should know, I have been warned. I'm aware your brother is Senator Clark."

"Odd you should say '*warned*' Mr. Goldman. It makes me curious about your choice of words." Mia shrugged. "My brother may be a senator, but I still have to work for a living, even if my brother is a politician. I'd appreciate your cooperation."

"Why pretend this isn't about your brother? You're digging around to find out what I know about his affair with Leigh Anne Saddler, right?"

"What affair," Mia had never been more proud of her acting ability than she was at that moment. With her emotions seething in response to his jabs, she still managed to force words through stiff lips. "I heard Leigh Anne Saddler was dating a company vice-president." Mia held her breath, anticipating his response, as she swirled the drink in her glass. Dim lighting and flickering shadows kept her from being certain, but color seemed to drain from Goldman's face.

"Where did you hear that nonsense?" Goldman barked a sound intended for a laugh as his gaze bored into her. "If that's your line of questioning, you're way off base."

"So, Leigh Anne didn't date Edward Poole?" Mia cocked her chin, challenging him to deny facts she could prove. "Just as a reminder, I will be quoting you in the article I'm writing for the paper. So before you answer, I should tell you I have two sources confirming that information. One of which is Edward Poole."

Goldman's eyes flickered fast as ticker tape before he dropped his glance to the glass clenched in fingers the cold slick color of a corpse. "That's right, I forgot about Edward. He's such a fool. He'll date anything in a skirt. Are you interested?" Taking a swallow of his drink, Goldman's gaze sliced over her to assess her reaction to his off color remark, then he returned to the reason for their meeting. "If you already have two sources, Ms Clark, then you don't need me."

Trying to stop him from clamming up and walking away, Mia

rushed to respond. "Actually, I have three sources. Your input would make four statements representing the company. I didn't want to leave your opinion out of my article."

"What are you trying to trick me into saying, Ms. Clark? Leigh Anne and Pam are both dead. I am sorry. The company will miss them very much. If you wanted to hear more than that, you're out of luck."

Mia's blood chilled under his frigid stare. "Is it true that you are the father of Leigh Anne's unborn child?"

"Who told you that?" Goldman demanded. He stepped so close his sleeve brushed against her breast, causing ice pellets to form in her blood as he growled. "The autopsy results haven't even been released, yet."

"Your influence, I'm sure." Mia angled her chin higher as she met his frigid glare.

"Are you accusing the police department of bribery and corruption, Ms. Clark? Is that how you acquired the autopsy results before they were released to the public?"

"I have sources. I don't need to wait for an announcement." Mia tilted her head high. "I have it on good authority that you had an affair with Leigh Anne Saddler. And that you sent her to seduce my brother."

If eyes could freeze, Mia would turn to a glacier under his glowering stare. Shoulders rigid, she returned Goldman's glare for long seconds, feeling her heart almost jump out of her chest.

Then Goldman barked a laugh. "Nice try, Ms. Clark. If you live long enough, with that imagination of yours, you'll make a good reporter."

"Is that a threat, Mr. Goldman?"

"No, young lady, I'm giving you advice. Hone your skills on local news and you might live to reach the top of your profession, such as it is." With one last sneer, Goldman wheeled and stomped away.

Knees wobbling, Mia gasped for air. Thomas Goldman had stared at her as if he wanted to choke the air out of her lungs, but that didn't make him a killer. She couldn't go to the police without evidence that Goldman had killed those two women. If she couldn't prove Goldman was the murderer, how could she clear Phil?

"Are you all right?" Jake bumped against her back and paused. To anyone in the crowd they looked like strangers bumping into each other in the crowd, but every fiber in Mia's body responded to Jake's strength. His protectiveness made her feel stronger.

"I'm fine. Freezing," she shivered in the cool night air, "but I'm okay. Can we go, now?"

"What about Yow?" Jake asked as they eased through the crowd.

Mia stopped mid-step and stared back at the crowd gathered around the outdoor bar. "I forgot about him. Do you think he's still here? Should we look for him?"

"He might be upstairs listening to the band." Jake took her arm and urged her forward. "We need to get out of here."

"Not together," Mia pushed away from his side, "he might be watching."

"Okay, but stay close." Jake warned as he turned and headed out of the gate to the sidewalk.

Mia followed about two yards behind him. She walked out the gate and about five strides down the street, when someone grabbed her from behind, clamped a hand over her mouth, and started dragging her toward the shadows.

She flung her arms and twisted, trying to grab hold of her captor, but nothing worked. Smothering from the gloved hand over her mouth and nose, darkness closed in on her. *Not again.* She couldn't disappear with Jake in sight…

Jake.

Images of Jake filled her fuzzy head. Strength surged through her body. She didn't want to lose Jake and her hopes for their future. And for what? To end up with her throat slashed like the other two women because of men like Goldman and Poole? Men willing to lie and cheat to get their way, no matter who they hurt. Jake was worth a dozen of those men. She wanted to spend her life with him. Escaping from this man right now, was her only hope.

Bending her right arm, Mia rammed a swift jab to the man's stomach with all the force she could muster.

"Sonofabitch." Her captor grunted and loosened his grip.

Mia hit the ground hard.

"Jake," she screamed, crawling away on her hands and knees as fast as she could. Shuffling and scrapping noises sounded on the pavement behind her and panic gripped her.

Then the sound of Jake's footsteps thundered the sidewalk. He rushed toward her and fell on his knees beside her. "Mia, what happened? Did you fall?"

Angered by his assumption that she was just clumsy, when she was certain she had just escaped from the killer, Mia shoved to her feet and forced words past gritted teeth. "Someone grabbed me from behind and covered my mouth so I couldn't scream."

"Are you sure?" Jake searched the dark shadows from trees and vehicles. "I was only a few feet ahead of you. I didn't hear anything."

Wanting to punch someone else in the middle, Mia stomped away, and headed in the direction of their vehicle. "You think I made this up?"

Jake's long legged stride brought him alongside her in a couple of steps. "Did you get a look at him?"

"No." She climbed in the car and slammed the door. "Let's get out of here. Someone might call the police."

"He must have been watching the whole time."

Her mouth dropped open as she turned to stare at him. "Yow?"

"Too convenient," Jake shook his head, but kept his eyes on the road, "and we saw him at *He Just Left*, but so was half the population of Chapel Hill."

"Okay, if it wasn't Yow. Who was it?" Hugging her arms across her chest, Mia stared out at the night. "I'm tired of people grabbing me from behind."

"Are you okay?" Jake glanced at her profile in the dimness of the Explorer's interior, then turned his attention back to the road. The twenty minutes since they left Chapel Hill had passed in silence.

Headlights dwindled as they traveled Hwy 15/501 out of town. Had the assailant hurt her? Frightened her?

"I'm relieved we got away before anyone called police." Mia wiggled in her seat.

"With the band playing that loud, we don't know if anyone even heard the commotion." Jake glanced away from the road. "Talking to the police might be a good idea."

Mia jerked around to face him. "We can't. I'm not hurt. They wouldn't believe me, anyway. The second they asked my name, they would start asking questions about Phil's relationship to Leigh Anne Saddler."

"We haven't had a chance to go over your conversation with Phil. Do you think he told you the truth?" After long moments of silence, Jake sent her a questioning glance. Her sigh sounded loud in the dark interior of the SUV. Jake reached over and put his hand on hers. "I know this is difficult. He's your brother. You love him. I get that, but ignore the emotions. Look at facts. Did Phil kill the model?"

"If he did," her voice wobbled. She paused, drawing a quivering breath. "And I don't think it's possible, but just for the sake of the argument. If he killed Leigh Anne, why would he admit to having an affair with her?"

"Passion? Arrogance?"

Mia swiped tears off her cheeks with her sleeve. "I don't understand how he could cheat on a wife and kids who love him? I-I can't believe he stooped that low."

"Try not to focus on that angle. You can deal with the personal issues after we solve the murders. We need to find out who wants to harm you."

"How can the police miss all these incidents? We're trying to be inconspicuous, but shouldn't someone notice these attacks?" Mia paused to catch her breath and hammered her fist on her thigh. "Even if I went to the police, I don't have one witness to back up my story."

"You have me." Jake arched a brow.

Mia snorted. "Right, a judge on the run and my partner in crime. Who is going to believe you? There's not one shred of evidence in our favor."

"Do you think Phil killed Leigh Anne?" Jake repeated.

"No," Mia's voice boomed loud in the SUV. "I told you. I don't believe that for a second. And you didn't answer my question. If you think Phil killed Leigh Anne, then who killed Pam Foley?"

Jake glanced in her direction, sensing her tension from the forward thrust of her head as she leaned toward him. Man, he did not like having to do this, but he had to sort the facts. "Phil said Pam seduced him. Maybe he killed both women."

"Great. Just great. You're the judge and the jury, now, are you?" Her words ripped through the darkness. "Phil said Pam was nice. He couldn't resist Leigh Anne's sex appeal. Does that sound like the words of a killer?"

Lifting a shoulder, Jake glanced away from the road. "People kill their spouse all the time, and they loved them at least long enough to marry them."

"Okay, Phil's words don't clear him. But I know him. He could- not commit murder." Mia sighed.

"You have doubts. Don't deny it. Remember the morning after the fire. We were searching for the disc. You were worried that Le- igh Anne might be telling the truth about Phil."

Mia slumped in her seat. "So? Phil admitted some of what Leigh Anne said was true. They had an affair. But he's certain he didn't get her pregnant."

"You believe him this time?" Jake hated saying the words. Hat- ed making her admit her brother had made bad choices, but her life was at risk. They didn't know who was trying to harm her. "He lied under oath at the hearing and committed prudery."

"Phil cheated on his wife, had two affairs—"

"Because he could—"

"What are you saying?" Mia whirled to face him. "Because he could...what?"

"Wait." Jake checked the rearview mirror and pulled out to pass a slow moving car. "We can't ignore the fact that Phil is a politi- cian. He does things ordinary men can't or won't do. It's part of his job description. We've been looking at this all wrong."

"What? We shouldn't blame him, since he's a politician?"

"No, ask yourself why it was so easy for him to cheat. Why did two women throw themselves at him? One was an ex-model, and he wasn't her first fling, but why Pam Foley?"

"Phil said she was the kind of woman you take home..." Mia turned wide eyes on Jake. "So, why did Pam throw herself at Phil? Why would someone with Leigh Anne's connections go after a man like Phil? He's a senator, sure, but he isn't Tom Selleck. Why would a former model have a fling with Phil?"

"Because she wanted something from him."

"Phil isn't rich or powerful. Someone used her to get to him." Mia's voice rose as she grabbed Jake's arm. "This all points back to Stern-McHamlin."

Jake nodded. "Both women were secretaries for the company,

and both were murdered."

"What did Stern-McHamlin want from Phil?" Mia's question echoed inside the dark car.

Chapter Fifteen

Whistling tunelessly as he considered her question, Jake stared at the road ahead. Few cars had stayed with them for the twenty miles back to the lakefront community. Glancing away from the road, he turned to look at Mia. "I think we can take Phil off the list of suspects."

"You're certain?"

The hopeful note in her voice tore at Jake's heart. Giving a left signal, he steered toward their exit. "Yeah, I think it's time. Who does that leave on the list?"

"The four vice-presidents. We should rank them. I would put Charles Herne at the bottom of the list."

"Fell for his blond good-looks did you?" Jake welcomed her loss of tension.

"He's really nice, and losing Leigh Anne broke his heart."

Jake slowed and turned right. "There's the entrance to the Tobacco Trail. I wondered where it came out."

Mia looked over her shoulder. "How long has that car been behind us?" Then she sniffed. "Listen to me. I'll be neurotic by the time this is over."

Jake stared in the rearview mirror. "I wish I could reassure you, but I didn't notice anything until he turned off behind us."

"It could be someone who went to a late movie." Mia looked in the side mirror. "It's not following close."

"Could be nothing." Jake returned his attention to the road.

"Back to the list. What is your best guess?"

Chewing on her lip, Mia watched mailboxes slip past their headlights. "I think Alan Yow is third. Edward Poole and Thomas Goldman are a toss-up."

"How do you figure?" Jake eased in the driveway and hit the garage remote.

"Well, Edward Poole is the spurned lover—"

"So is Charles Herne."

"Yes, but Charles Herne really seems broken up about Leigh Anne's death."

Jake laughed and shook his head as he climbed out of the SUV.

"What?" Mia demanded standing in the open passenger door and staring at him across the bucket seats. "Don't laugh. Charles Herne is mourning Leigh Anne's death. Poole and Goldman don't seem to care."

Jake braced a hand on the headrest and stared at her through the car. "Which one gave you bad vibes?"

Eyes sparkling with laughter, Mia leaned her elbow on the back of the passenger seat and looked across the interior at him. "So, is this how a judge's mind works? You decide your cases on gut instinct?"

Jake shrugged. His gaze roamed over her laughter-filled face. Mia's smile made his pulse race. He wanted to see more of that smile. Wanted to make her laugh and enjoy life.

Whoa.

What was he thinking? When this was over, he wouldn't have any reason to see more of Mia. They would say goodbye and go their separate ways. But he didn't want that. He wanted Mia in his life. An hour ago, someone had tried to kidnap her. Before he could think about the future, he had to make sure she got out of this alive.

"Sometimes, instinct is your best bet." Jake swallowed as he looked in her eyes. "If I had listened to my wife's feelings, she might not have died."

Mia expelled an audible breath. "What happened?"

Slumping against the outside of the car, Jake leaning on the seat and met her gaze. "There was a firefighting training session in Raleigh that weekend. I wanted to go. She asked me not to go." He shrugged. "I went, so she and Stevie went to the movies alone. If I had stayed home like she asked, I would have been driving and they might still be alive."

"Or you might be dead, too." Mia's heart ached for the pain she saw in his eyes. "It wasn't your fault, Jake. You couldn't have prevented the accident."

"I know that in my heart, but the question is always there in my head, the wondering—"

Bright lights suddenly glared through the small windows at the top of the garage doors behind them. A loud engine sounded on the other side of the door. She thought the vehicle was going to ram into the doors. "What—"

Jake leaned further in the cab so she could hear him and his eyes bored into hers. "You can't say this isn't my fault. I should have kept better check on the traffic behind us."

Mia glanced toward the garage doors, then back to his face. "Maybe it's your friend, Dan."

Shaking his head, Jake cut a glance toward the sudden silence as the engine stopped. The car's lights went out, leaving the interior bulb of the SUV as the only light in the garage. They had been so intent on debating the guilt of the vice-presidents they hadn't turned on the lights in the garage.

"Check the glove box for a flashlight," Jake said as he latched his door quietly, and crossed to her side.

"Nothing," Mia murmured as she backed out of the passenger door.

"Latch the door to kill the light and stay here." Jake murmured against her cheek. Then he moved toward the automatic doors. Once there, he looked out the high windows."It's a black sports car."

Mia's heart thumped so loud she almost didn't hear his whisper. "How did he find us?"

Jake took her shoulders in his hands and gave her a gentle squeeze. "My guess is he followed us home."

"But how...you don't think it—"

"The same person who grabbed you outside the bar? Yeah." He pulled her against his chest and wrapped her so tight in his arms, their hearts beat as one.

Mia melted against him. When she imagined being close enough to feel a man's heart beat in tune with hers, she had expected it to be an act of affection or passionate lovemaking. *Love. Passion. Intimacy.* She wanted those things with Jake. But they were in a garage and the person on the other side the door wanted them dead.

Instead of the dream scenario of her imagination, she had fear, threats, and danger. Gulping for air, she stared up at the shadow of Jake's head. "What are we going to do?"

"He drove in and didn't try to conceal his presence. He means business." Jake whispered.

"Why didn't he sneak in so the neighbors wouldn't see him?" Mia breathed the words into the dark.

Jake's grip on her shoulders tightened. "He's desperate. He doesn't want us to escape. He pulled his car close, blocking both garage doors."

Mia gasped. "We're trapped?"

"For the moment." Jake gave her a quick hug and held her away. "It all comes down to this, Mia. Are you ready to finish this battle?"

Mia recalled all the fear, worry, and danger they had experienced since the fire. "I want to know who is trying to kill me."

"He's going around the house. My guess is he'll try to break in."

"Why doesn't he just wait for us to come out?" She heard the plea in her words. Waiting sounded good.

"We might call the police." Jake murmured.

"We could. We have the phones." She fumbled for her jeans pocket, but Jake stopped her with a hand over hers.

"By the time police arrived this far out of town, we could be dead and this guy long gone." He squeezed her shoulder. "We have to get out of this on our own."

"How? We can't drive out. If we run, he'll catch us in the car." She felt Jake stiffen at her side. Then she heard it too. The sound of glass breaking. "He's at the sliding glass doors in the den, isn't he?"

"Yeah," Jake tugged on her arm. "Come on, our time just ran out. If he doesn't find us in the house, he'll check out here. We'll be sitting ducks."

Legs trembling, she followed Jake to the far side of the garage. He stopped. She strained to see in the dark as he let go her arm.

She heard his grunt of satisfaction.

"I thought I remembered seeing bicycles."

"Bicycles? Are you crazy? It's dark out there. How can we ride..."

Jake shoved handlebars into her hands. "How can we not?"

Mia looked at the shadowy outline of a bike and shook her head. "How will we see?"

He leaned close and whispered. "Follow me to the corner. There's a single door there. Move as quiet as you can. We don't have a second to waste."

Knees knocking as if this were her first bicycle ride ever, Mia followed and eased her bike out the door behind him.

Jake turned left, staying behind the wall of the garage, instead of heading for the street. Mia followed, praying they would escape with their lives. Jake turned down the neighbor's driveway and hopped on his bike.

Mia climbed on her bike and pedaled to catch up with him. The cold bright moon gave enough light to find their way, but she wished they could see better. They were still in sight of the house when she heard a crash behind them. Was it the sound of breaking glass or a gunshot?

She pumped the pedals faster.

"Don't stop," Jake called softly. "Follow me, I have a head-light."

Follow me! How many times had she heard those words?

Even as she battled the urge to scream, panic clamped the sound in her throat. As she rounded the curve in the street, she noticed the dim light in front of Jake's bike. He really did have a light. Some-how, that dim yellow glow gave her a ray of hope that they could escape this madman.

They were streaking down the tobacco trail before Mia realized they could have gone to a neighbor's house. "Why didn't we go next door and call police?"

Jake dropped back beside her. "Keep your voice down. Sound travels at night. We couldn't take the risk. We're strangers. Neigh-bors might not believe us, and even if they did, by stopping we would put their lives at risk." He pulled ahead. "Come on, we can do this."

For about five minutes, Mia believed him. They could do this.

Then she caught a flash of light out of the corner of her eye. Risking a wreck, she glanced over her shoulder, and saw a light similar to the one on Jake's bike.

No. It couldn't be.

A few yards later, she looked back again. The light was still there. Closer, even.

"Jake," she panted as she tried to catch up with him. "We have a problem."

"Yeah, I saw the light. Pedal fast as you can so we can gain a lead on him." Jake pumped his powerful legs and sent his bike rolling away.

Mia's heart thumped in her chest. The cold air brought tears to her eyes and made it hard to breathe. The muscles in her legs screamed at the new demands put on her body.

With Jake leading, she kept her gaze on his back tire and followed as close as she could. The tobacco trail might be a delight for cyclists in the daytime, but on a cold March night, it was not her idea of fun. But she wanted to escape the killer and live another day. She couldn't let Jake down.

Chapter Sixteen

If she slowed up, Jake would, too. She would put both of them in danger. She had started this search by telling herself she couldn't quit. Now, she really couldn't, her life was on the line, not Phil's career. She had put Jake at risk, as well. Fueled with renewed energy, she pedaled with a renewed burst of speed.

She wanted...Jake and a future. She couldn't allow a madman to cheat her of a chance spend time with Jake now that she'd found him. Eyes on his back wheel, her feet on the pedals, she intended to go as far as needed to escape.

"Mia."

Focused on pedaling, she didn't hear her name until Jake called a second time.

"Mia, stop."

"Did we loose him?" She asked, panting.

"He's gaining. We just rode over a culvert. Let's go back."

Mia followed him and stared at a black hole under the trail.

Jake dropped his bike to the ground. Grabbed her bike and rolled it behind a large bush.

Brow puckered, Mia stared. "What—"

"No time to explain." Jake motioned to the dark shadow at his feet. "Climb in."

Mia's heart stopped. She bent closer and looked in the knee-high culvert. It was totally black. "I can't—"

"It's our only chance. I'll lead him away and come back to get you." Jake urged her into the black hole. "Lie down and back in. If you hear something, don't move. I'll come back for you." At the last second, he pressed a hard kiss to her lips then pushed her to the ground.

Her lips tingling from his kiss, Mia bit back a whimper and stared at the culvert running under the bike trail. What if she got stuck...as she had as a kid? What if the slasher got Jake? What if he couldn't come back to get her? What if...

"Hurry, he's getting closer. I have to go."

The urgency in his words ended her mental battle. It was time she learned to control her emotions. This was a matter of life and death. Hers and Jake's. She could do this.

"It's wet." She shivered as water in the bottom of the culvert soaked her jeans.

"I'll be back as soon as I can." Jake grabbed his bike. Gravel crunched as he wheeled back on the trail.

She started to scramble after him. Then saw the tiny light approaching fast. Fighting fears she'd had all her life, she wiggled backwards into the dark culvert.

Her head and shoulders brushed against the walls. Her breath came fast and shallow so she almost passed out from fright, but the few inches of space over her head kept her from screaming. The tight, black space, dank odor, and the unknown person chasing them, added to emotions almost crushing her chest.

Memories played in her head in 3-D color. She'd been four. A skinny little kid without fear, when new floor covering for the kitchen arrived in a long cardboard roll. After workers emptied the tube, she and Phil claimed the cardboard tunnel for a toy. On the last of many trips crawling through the dark tube, she had gotten stuck.

Lying in the cold wet culvert, sweat beads pop out on her forehead. Her childhood panic flared to new life. As a child, she hadn't been able to wiggle backward, or go forward. After her father cut her free, Mia learned Phil had been riding the tube like a horse. His weight collapsed the tube in front of her face. To this day, closed dark spaces instilled terror in her.

And this culvert was dark. On the verge of hyperventilating, she forced her thoughts to Jake and the danger he had risked to save her. Forcing deep breaths into her lungs to keep from passing out, she focused on the current threat to their safety.

The sound of crunching gravel sent new fears exploding in her head and catching at her throat. She held her breath until dots danced in front of her eyes. She inhaled, expecting the culvert to collapse on her as the cardboard tunnel had... She listened. The to sound of crunching gravel got closer. Louder.

With her heart almost jumping out of her chest, sanity returned. The noise of bicycle wheels on the small gravel layering the bike trail reminded her of their remote location. Jake told her to stay hidden to keep her safe, but what about him.

New fears entered her head.

What if the madman saw her bike in the bushes and stopped? She dug her fingers into the wet cold surface of the culvert and fought the urge to crawl out.

Would the slasher find her?

If he stopped, there was no way she could escape.

She couldn't go further back in the wet sludge...then Jake's words, asking her to stay out of sight, echoed in her head, and kept her in place. Jake was risking his life to protect her. She had to do as he'd asked.

The crunching sounded over her head and echoed in the culvert. Then, fast as it came, the sound faded away, disappearing in the direction Jake had gone.

Inhaling deep breaths of cold, smelly air in the culvert, new fears exploded in her head. What if the madman caught up with Jake, and she wasn't there to help him. What if Jake couldn't return to tell her it was safe? What if she waited and...

Adrenaline sent her slithering out of the culvert into the cold moonlit night. She was alive. Wet. Cold. Stinky, but she was alive. And she intended to stay that way, shivering limbs and all. It was time to make sure Jake stayed safe as well.

Staring in the direction Jake and the madman had ridden, flashes of white sent fear slamming against her ribs.

Those white blurs weren't coming from the headlamp on the bike. The flashes were low to the ground and moving up and down. Instantly, she realized she was watching the stark white of shoes in the moonlight as the madman peddled after Jake.

Terror clogged her throat. She had faced fears of the dark by climbing in that culvert and survived. She wanted Jake to know that. He wouldn't have a chance if the man following him had his way. She recalled the man's strength and willingness to inflict pain.

A flash of anger overshadowed her fright. In a split second, she ran for her bike and wasted precious seconds steering out of the bushes and back to the trail. With an urgency fueled by the pumping of her heart, she raced to assist Jake.

Never mind that he told her to wait for his return. She knew this madman's intentions. She could feel the pain on her head from his rough grip when he tried to abduct her outside Grover's.

She couldn't let Jake face the danger alone.

�🚲

Jake saw the light behind was gaining on him. He had lost time trying to comfort Mia, but he had determination on his side. He would not give their pursuer a chance to hurt her. If he had to ride the twenty miles to Durham to lead the man away, he would.

Then a thought exploded in his head, almost causing his legs to stop moving. Had the man chasing him spotted Mia's bicycle behind the bushes? Had he found Mia's hiding place?

Looking back over his shoulder, Jake lost precious time trying to judge the location of the pursuer's headlight. He could ride with the best cyclists around, but keeping one eye on the pursuer, to make sure he was following and not stopping for Mia, cut his lead.

He shouldn't have left her.

He should have hidden the bikes in the bushes and waited for the attacker to ride past. He wanted this to end. He was tired of trying to stay one-step ahead of a killer. But if they had waited for the bad guy to ride past, they would be watching over their shoulders for who knows how long.

This way, he could lead the killer into a trap. But what kind of trap could he set? He was convinced the man behind him was the murderer. The bike trail was closed to the public at night. There wouldn't be other riders to offer assistance, and no park employees checking for safety. He was in this on his own.

He had to protect Mia.

He wanted a chance for more than just protecting Mia. He wanted to spend his future with her. He wanted to wrap her in his arms and keep her safe. Memories of failing his wife flashed through his head.

What was he thinking?

He'd left Mia in the dark, alone. The killer could find her, murder her and rob Jake of the second woman he loved. He couldn't face that loss, that sense of failure, again. Give him a battle, and he would fight, but losing Mia after finding hope, would kill him.

Without stopping to reconsider his decision, Jake wheeled the bicycle around and rode at top speed back the way he had come.

He had to check on Mia. If anything happened to her...

The shadowy figure came at him like a bat out of the sky. One second Jake was pedaling fast to reach Mia. The next second he landed flat of his back, winded and shaken by the collision of the two bikes.

He heard gravel scattering and the grinding noise of metal scrapping as the bicycles fell to the ground. He tried to catch his breath, but a huge dark shadow swooped down and landed on his chest.

Jake felt the blow to his chin the same instant he realized the shadowy figure seemed so large because the attacker was wearing a hood over his head.

Was this the same man who tried to abduct Mia? Another blow landed on his face and sent pain vibrating though his head. Spots danced in front of his eyes. He swung at the covered head, and connected with a blow. He heard a grunt from the man on top of him and swung again as he rolled to the side.

But his assailant stayed on top of him like a bronco rider. Jake bucked and twisted to get free, but the man clung to his back. The attacker's legs squeezed against his ribs. His weight pushed Jake's body into the gravel. The attacker grabbed a handful of hair on the back of Jake's head and slammed his face to the ground.

Jake tried to reach behind him for a grip on the man's clothing, but he grasped thin air. Another blow slammed his face into the gravel, again. New worries exploded in his head with the pain.

If he couldn't fight off this assailant, how could Mia? He had to protect her. The need to guard Mia renewed his strength. He gave another twist and rolled away from the man clinging to his back, but his few seconds of freedom ended when another blow struck his chin.

Jake fell into nothingness. His last thought was the realization that he had lost Mia, too.

Mia heard the grunts before she picked out the figures tangled in deep shadows beside the trail. Stumbling off the bike, she ran toward them. Her wet jeans stuck to her legs, making it hard to move. But she had to help Jake.

Skittering to a halt, she saw the hooded figure take powerful swing at Jake's head as the two men scuffled on the ground.

Oh, Jake.

Jake was trapped under the slasher's weight. She heard the crunching noise as Jake's head hit the ground. Fury built inside her with the speed of a tornado. Frantic to help Jake, she searched the ground for some object to give her an advantage over the attacker.

A long shadow at the edge of the trail looked like a broken limb. Mia stared for a second, praying it wasn't a snake. By the time her common sense told her it was too cold for snakes, she had a grip on the rough bark of the limb.

Even then, she paused, unaccustomed to inflicting bodily harm on another person, but the hooded figure on top of Jake had no qualms. His next blow to Jake's face sounded like a crack of thunder.

Her fury returned. Fueled by her need to save Jake, she drew the limb back over her shoulder and swung the limb like a baseball bat, as hard as she could. Like a slow motion movie, she saw her arm extend and move forward as the man's fist landed another thudding blow to Jake's face.

In the last instant before the limb hit, she saw Jake's head fall back. His body wilted into the gravel. Then she noticed the stark white athletic shoe resting at Jake's side and fear took over.

At the last second, she stumbled. The limb struck the slasher a glancing blow across the shoulders. He let out a yelp and slumped over. In a blink, Mia landed on his back.

The slasher twisted around and grabbed a handful of her hair. Pain sliced through her scalp as he jerked her up and wrapped a hand around her neck.

Mia twisted, kicked and punched out at him, but she couldn't loosen his grip on her throat. Air left her lungs. Staring in the gargoyle features of the slasher's shadowy face, Mia knew she might never see Jake again.

Her last thoughts were of never feeling his kisses again, or having a chance to tell him she really meant it when she told him she loved him. Then darkness swallowed her.

Chapter Seventeen

*F*ire.
A coffin.

She was trapped alive and moving steadily toward the fire that would turn her body to ashes. She tried to fight, to get out, to move, but she couldn't escape. She tried to see, but everything was black.

She was trapped in a coffin. She was going to die. Who put her in this box, alive? Why? Who had she harmed?

The stench of smoke filled Mia's nostrils and pulled her out of the nightmare and back to consciousness. She sucked air in her lungs and with each breath, she became more alert.

The movement she had felt was her head hanging down.

She became aware of the smell of smoke and coughed, winching at the pain in her head. Chills shook her body, but even though she struggled, she couldn't move. Squinting down at her body, she saw her arms were pulled behind the tree at her back, and her hands tied. Blinking against the sickening pain when she moved, she forced her head up and stared through smoke surrounding her. Was she back in the courthouse again?

No. Where was she? Where was Jake?

Then, through the wispy plumes of smoke, she saw him. He was about four feet away, and tied upright against a tree. His head hung to his chest. The rope around his feet and hands held him upright, but she couldn't tell if he was breathing.

Was he alive?

"Jake!" Her hoarse whisper scraped her throat. Looking again, she realized she was tied in the same position as Jake, and a roaring blaze burned close in the brush behind them.

She struggled against the rope, trying to loosen her hands, but nothing happened.

She couldn't move.

Smoke filled her nostrils and lungs.

Her old nightmare flashed through her head like a horror movie, but this was not a dream.

This was real. She wasn't in a coffin, but still at risk of burning alive.

This new danger was worse than any dream.

If she and Jake couldn't escape, no one would know who had burned them alive.

Twisting and tugging, she pulled against the rope. And twisted. Turned. Pulled. But she couldn't free her hands.

Coughing against the clogged air, she stared at Jake through the smoke. He looked so helpless, hanging against the tree, with his head drooping. Pain squeezed her chest. How could their future end like this? Jake was all she had ever dreamed of finding in a man she could love. And the slasher was stealing her dreams.

Anger and pain twisted inside her. Love for Jake surged through her. Teeth gritted, she tugged at the rope on her hands with new strength.

Wiggling pulled the rope tighter. She tried to bend her knees to move her body down the tree, but the way her feet were tied, she couldn't move.

The wind blew smoke in her face and plastered her wet jeans against her legs. The chill felt good after hearing the blaze burning behind her.

"Jake!" She couldn't see behind her to check how close the fire was, but she felt the heat. Heard the snapping and crackling, and smelled the smoke. Panic grew inside her.

"Jake?" She had to wake him, needed his help, needed to warn him of the danger. "Jake!"

She heard the pain and fear in her voice, and fought for control.

Control.

The one thing she had never achieved. First her parents, and then her mother's ambitions for Phil had taken charge of Mia's existence. She loved her family, but it was time for her to take charge.

She had survived the culvert...her jeans were soggy and she smelled worse than wet gym shoes, but she had crawled out of that culvert in one piece. She had fought her fear of the dark and won. She would fight her fear of fire and save Jake.

She was his only hope.

The fire crackled closer.

She tried to think of a plan. Flames burned brush littering the ground and danced around her feet. The blaze was close enough to make her jeans steam, but she didn't feel pain.

Then...watching the steam, a solution popped in her head.

Was she brave enough? Desperate enough?

Jake moaned.

She was more than desperate. She was in love with Jake. She had to save him.

"Jake." She stared through the smoke. His body sagged from the tree, but he didn't respond. "Jake? Can you hear me? We have to get free from this rope or we will burn alive."

Rope!

Now she remembered. She'd seen the rope coiled over the slasher's shoulder when she hit him with the limb. He had come prepared.

She started shaking. The slasher had planned the way he wanted them to die. Why? She didn't even know who he was.

Images of that encounter came back in a flash. She had swung the limb at his head. At the last second, he raised his arm and the limb landed a glancing blow to the coiled rope. Then the shadowy figure had whirled on her.

Now she knew how they ended up tied to trees.

But she had to figure a way to get them free. The years she spent in fear of burning alive, became a reality as the sound of the blaze came closer. "Jake!"

It was no use. She had witnessed his beating. She had been too late to help him fight off the slasher. She had to help him now. There was no other choice if she wanted to get out of this alive.

Looking through the smoke at Jake's sagging figure, she remembered how he had protected her since the day they met. Now, he was unconscious and she had to save him.

One of them had to survive to tell police what they'd learned.

Fighting back panic, she focused on the heat at her feet. Her socks and jeans were wet from the culvert, but the rope wasn't. If she could ignore the warmth on her skin, maybe the rope would burn.

Closing her eyes tight, she focused on questions. Tried to reason out the slasher's plan, anything to keep from thinking about the fire burning close to her body.

Why had the slasher taken time to tie them up? To avoid any chance one of them might regain consciousness and get the other to safety. Seemed reasonable.

But why here?

Why on the bike trail? Because they had dashed this way to escape, making it easy to dispose of them. They were in a deep wooded section of the trail. The twenty-mile trail, converted railroad tracks, provided a close glimpse of nature.

Too, close, this time.

Was the slasher still out there? Why had he slashed their throats as he had the two women? Why wait? Was he coming back? If he returned, he could end her attempts to escape. If he knocked her out again, she and Jake would both die in the flames.

Then she felt it.

The pressure holding her feet against the tree, eased.

She wiggled and realized her feet were free. The rope had burned through...but she wasn't free. Her hands were tied behind her.

The wet jeans had protected her legs, but nothing would protect her hands while flames destroyed the rope. She had to try...had to face her fear of burning if she wanted to escape. Jake's life depended on her actions.

It was now or never.

If she passed out from pain, maybe she would fall forward enough to keep from burning...but commonsense told her delaying wouldn't make the situation any better. No white knight was going to ride up and cut her loose. She had to risk being burned to make her escape and save Jake.

Squeezing her eyes tight, teeth sinking in her lip, she slithered down the tree.

Heat flared around her hands. The instinct to jerk away was so strong she could barely resist, but now that she was sitting on the ground, she didn't have a choice. Taking a deep breath, she pulled her wrists as far apart as she could and waited.

Images from her nightmares flashed through her head. Memories of burning her hand as a kid flashed in her mind. *What if...*

Then, miraculously, her hands fell free. She tumbled forward, landing on her face and knees in the leaves and twigs on the ground. Jerking upright, she slapped at the smoke coming from the sleeves of her sweat jacket. Thank heavens polyester melted instead of burning.

Her hands ached. In the dim light from the flames, she couldn't see the burns but that wasn't her main problem. Flames were two feet from Jake's tree. She had to get him untied.

"Jake? Can you hear me? Please wake up. I need to get you away from this fire."

"Don't move," Jake whispered. "He might still be out there."

"Oh, Jake." She bit back a sob, and voice quivering, she said the words searing in her head. "I thought we were going to burn alive."

"We aren't out of the woods, yet." Jake winched. "If he's watching, we're still in danger. I'll keep an eye out in front, you keep watch behind me."

She attacked the knot in the ropes at his feet, but the pain in her fingers made her feel faint. "I can't untie the knot at your feet. My hands are burned."

"Burn the rope off like you did yours."

"You were awake? Why didn't you say something?"

"Don't look at me." He cautioned. "I couldn't help you, so I kept watch."

Picking up a burning limb, she smothered a gasp of pain, and held the flame to the rope at his feet. "The next part is tricky. I have to get your hand free."

"I'm not going anywhere," Jake reminded her, with a glance out of the corner of his eyes.

Lip clenched between her teeth, she held the flame close to the bindings on his wrist. With the knot in the middle, she had to burn through the thickest part to avoid contact with his skin. Even then, she worried she would burn him. The pain in her hands cautioned her to avoid that possibility.

If Jake flinched, she didn't notice. After long moments, the rope gave way. His hands were free. Mia dropped the limb and rushed around the tree. "Let me help you."

Jake clamped back a groan and straightened. "I'm okay. Keep alert. If he's watching, he knows we're free."

"What are we going to do?" She searched the darkness surrounding the fire. "Do you think he is waiting for us in the dark?"

Jake took her in a careful grip and examined her hands. "Your burns aren't as bad as I feared." He stared in her eyes. "Can you last a little longer?"

Biting her lip, Mia gave a nod.

Jake pulled out his phone. "It's time to talk to the police, agreed?"

Staring at him for long speaking seconds, Mia tipped her head in agreement.

Jake held her gaze as he called nine-one-one to report the blaze. Then he called his friend at the police station.

"Chief? It's Jake. Sorry it's so late, but the murderer made another attempt. This time he tried to burn me at the stake. I called the fire in to nine-one-one."

Mia's knees almost crumpled under her as Jake answered the chief's questions. Was the slasher still out there? Was he watching? Would he attack them again?

"We believe we have a suspect." Jake watched as Mia leaned against a tree. "Thomas Goldman."

He frowned at the phone. "Yes, the big wig with Stern-Mc-Hamlin. This isn't your jurisdiction, but I thought you would know who to call."

Turning the phone off, Jake stared at the fire. "I can't walk away and leave this blaze. Can you sit by that tree for a few minutes?"

Twisting a limb off an evergreen tree, Jake beat the flames. His attempts seemed futile, at first, but he made progress, except for the hottest portion of the blaze.

The stench of smoke, the ache in her hands and her stinging eyes reminded Mia of her past fears. Thinking of her efforts to get free the past few minutes, she realized she was stronger than her fears. She had faced the darkness of the culvert and crawled out.

She had held her hands to a blaze to burn her bindings free.

She had faced her nightmares and won. She had saved Jake. Did she dare pursue her feelings for him and risk rejection?

The person trying to kill them was still out there. She couldn't stop fighting until he was caught. Was it Thomas Goldman? Why?

She stared into the darkness, watching. "Will they arrest us?"

Jake stood on the opposite side of the fire. The assailant hadn't put a lot of effort into setting the blaze. He had tossed sticks in a pile behind the trees, and left the leaves on the forest floor to do the rest. Recent rains had left the leaves damp and not easy to burn.

"I don't think so." He winched. "If my face looks like it feels, police will know we didn't do this to ourselves."

The first responders arrived on four-wheelers. Two with fire-fighters and a third with EMTs. The firefighters rushed into action instantly, forcing Jake to turn to the medics.

The EMT examined Mia's hands and applied ointment.

The second EMT examined Jake. "You need x-rays. Are you seeing double? Dizzy? Nauseous?"

Jake answered no and the EMTs drove them out to the highway where a uniformed officer waited for them. "Come with me."

Chapter Eighteen

Hours later, a nurse rolled Mia's wheelchair out of the emergency room. "I can walk."

"You're injured. Let someone look after you for a while." When she wheeled Mia in the waiting room, half the occupants in the room jumped to their feet.

Jake came toward her, a metal brace taped to his nose so he looked like raccoon robot, with the bandages on his face.

"Are you okay?" he demanded the instant he reached her side.

Mia nodded. "Are you? I hope I look better than you do."

"Don't worry," He grinned and winced. "Firefighters are tougher than they look."

"Oh, Mia! I was so worried." Her mother pushed past Jake and leaned down to hug her shoulders. "You are always so reckless."

"Mother?" Mia started to remind her mother that she had started this whole thing. Then Phil, Ellen and their two kids, stepped close to the wheelchair. "How long have all of you been here?"

"We came as soon the police called." Phil gave her a one armed hug and stepped back. Ellen moved close to give Mia a watery smile, and whispered, "Thank you." The kids hung back, staring at the bandages on her hands.

Phil wrapped his arm around Ellen's shoulders. "We had a long talk while we waited. Ellen says if you could risk your life for me, she thinks I must be worth a second chance. Thanks, sis."

Blinking tears from her eyes, Mia opened her mouth, but no words came. Her mother stepped close to Mia and filled in the silence. "It's my fault, Mia. I shouldn't have called you for help."

"The thing is, sis, you've always been the strong one." Phil's voice was low. Only Mia and Jake and the family gathered around her chair could hear. "If I had been more like you, none of this would have happened."

Mia made a face. "You must be kidding? You are the one with a family, a wife and kids that love you. I want what you have, Phil. Don't ruin it."

"Mia, promise me you won't take risks like this ever again." Her mother urged. "I don't know what I would do if anything happened to you. Since your father died, you're the one I turn to. Phil has Ellen, the kids and his career to worry about. I've poured all my worries on you." Tears filled her eyes. "Promise you'll be more careful."

"Mia Clark?" A uniformed police officer, standing in the doorway, demanded in a loud voice. Everyone in the waiting room turned to stare. "Chief wants to see you and Jake Stone, downtown."

Mia waved to her family, noting the perplexed expressions on their faces as Jake wheeled her toward the exit.

Funny, how those closest to you go separate ways, but in an emergency, you can always count on your family.

🚲

Three hours later, the chief of police returned to the interrogation room.

"Goldman claims he didn't kill the model. DNA results won't be back for two days. What makes you so sure he's the one who tried to kill you?" He pulled out a chair on the opposite side of the table and sat down. There were bags under his eyes and wrinkles in his suit from the long day.

"I studied all the files I collected on the four vice-presidents and my interviews with them. I interviewed Pam Foley the night she died. I confronted my brother and all the evidence points to one of the vice presidents. I think Thomas Goldman is the father of Leigh Anne Saddler's baby." Mia tried to keep her tone level and not sound like a recording, but it was hard after repeating the same information for hours.

"Level with me, Ms. Clark. If your notes had pointed to your brother, would you have turned him in?"

"Thankfully, I didn't have to make that decision. Phil made mistakes, but he didn't kill anyone."

The chief waved a hand. "Yeah, that's what Goldman said before he lawyered up. Now, he won't say a word."

"You let him go?" Mia almost banged her hand on the table. "You can't."

"Innocen—"

"Until proven guilty," Mia snapped. "I want to leave."

The chief leaned across the table, bringing his fleshy face near hers. "There's a little matter of trespassing and this evidence you claim to have."

Her head started swimming. "I've been attacked twice and nearly burned alive, twice. Are you seriously going to talk about trespassing?"

"What about your evidence?"

"The cigarette butts we saved for DNA and my computer are in the lake house where we were hiding."

His breath spewed out. "This isn't over, Ms. Clark. We'll talk when the test results come back. In the meantime, don't leave town."

Chapter Nineteen

Mia turned to look at Jake as he drove out of Durham in the car Phil loaned them. "Should you be driving? You might have a concussion."

Jake braked for a car slowing to make a turn. "You can't drive with those bandages. That leaves me." He glanced across the console at her. "You should be in bed. What's so important that it can't wait until daylight?"

Mia sighed. They had left the police station at four-thirty in the morning. A ribbon of pink marked the horizon toward the east. If she hadn't taken painkillers, she might have agreed to wait until day, but the chief's warning had put her on edge.

"The chief didn't believe my story." She turned in the seat so she could see Jake. "I need to get the files on my computer. I just hope the slasher didn't beat us to it."

"The chief came down on you pretty hard, didn't he?" Jake pushed down on the gas. "At least it's over."

"He warned me he's going to call me back in when Goldman's DNA results return." She stared at Jake's profile for long seconds. "Was he rough on you?"

"Let's just say he wasn't pleased with my actions and leave it at that." He turned the car in the driveway and parked. The house belonging to Dan's parents looked normal. From the front, there was no sign of the broken glass they had heard when the slasher broke in. "At least he moved the car."

"You don't think he's still here, do you?" Mia's heart started racing as she stared at the house in the gray dawn light.

"I don't think so. If he attacked now, a jogger might see him and call the cops." Jake pulled the key out of the Lexus and opened his door. "Wait, I'll help you out."

Mia huffed with annoyance, but her hands were bandaged. Jake opened the door and leaned to unfasten her seatbelt. He was close enough to kiss. She studied the bruises on his face and lifted a bandaged hand to his cheek. He looked as tired and battered as she felt. "Jake, I—"

"Let's grab our things and get some breakfast." Jake said in his firm courtroom voice. "We can talk later."

Mia's hopes for more from him dwindled. "Sure, this won't take but a minute." Looking down at her hands, she sighed.

"I'll go in first and look around." He eased the side door to the garage open and checked around the cars.

Mia stood with her back to the door and watched the yard, hoping none of the neighbors chose that moment to look out their windows. She and Jake were being cautious to stay safe. To an onlooker their actions might appear suspicious.

"I don't see anything." Jake said from the other side of the cars.

Mia eased in. "I can't lock this door."

Jake appeared at her side and locked the door. "Stay behind me, just in case."

Opening the door leading to the kitchen, Jake looked around and motioned her inside as he whispered. "Be careful where you step. There's glass everywhere."

She stared at the shattered sliding doors. Shards of glass covered furniture and the floor. "I can leave the clothes, but I need my computer."

She eased over the glass, taking her time. Even being cautious, she wobbled like a toddler taking her first steps, but she finally reached the front of the sofa. She was so caught up in examining the destruction to the room, she forgot their danger until...

"Where it that computer," a deep voice demanded from the shadows on the other side of the room.

Mia gasped as a dim figure stepped out of the dark leading to hall. He was pointing a gun at her, but she couldn't see his face. Her knees trembled. Her first instinct was to run, but Jake was hidden in the dark shadows. She fought to keep from looking to check that he was okay, but the slasher didn't seem to know Jake was on the other side of the room.

Determined the murderer wouldn't win, she forced out words sounding braver than she felt. "You should know. You're the one who broke in."

"Don't play cute with me. I came back to get those files of yours. Since you managed to escape my little bonfire, you can hand over the files in person. Where's your boyfriend?"

"Why would I give you the files?" Mia ignored his last question. Out of the corner of her eye, she saw Jake's shadow move.

"Ah, still stubborn. What if I promise to let you go if you cooperate?" Sarcasm coated each word as he stepped further into the room.

Chills chased along Mia's spine as the slasher stepped closer. But knowing she was about to see the face of the killer kept her feet stuck to the floor. He wouldn't show his face and let her live. But she had too much to lose. She couldn't die. "Why are you following me? Why try to kidnap me?"

"Your luck has run out, Ms. Clark. Give me the files." He waved the gun in his hand. "Why didn't you heed the warnings I left on your doorstep?"

"You killed my neighbor's cat? Did you slash my tires, too?"

His laugh echoed with madness. "Nice touch, don't you think?"

"Did you murder Leigh Anne Saddler?" Mia squinted in the dim light, trying to see his face. "How did you get her body inside the courthouse?"

"Where's the boyfriend?" The slasher demanded.

It took all her willpower to keep from glancing over to make sure Jake was safe. "Why did you kill Pam Foley? What did she have to do with—"

"Pam stuck her nose in where it didn't belong." He snarled in a threatening tone. "She caught me going through Leigh Anne's computer files after she died."

"You're one of the bosses. You can look at any company file you wanted. Why kill Pam?" Mia mentally crossed her fingers, but she was certain this was one of the vice-presidents. It wasn't Edward Poole. The voice wasn't slimy enough. And it wasn't Thomas Goldman. So, she'd been wrong about him killing Leigh Anne.

That left two vice presidents. Every instinct she possessed wanted to believe Charles Herne had told her the truth when he said he loved Leigh Anne. That left one man. The man determined to kill her. Alan Yow.

"You didn't have to kill her, Mr. Yow."

"Ah, so you figured out it was me. You didn't tell police. They picked up Goldman." Yow waved the gun again. "I should have taken care of you that day in the courthouse." He stepped closer as he promised. "Don't worry. I'll finish the job as soon as you give me those files."

"Why bother with the files?" Mia forced back her shivers in reaction to his words and hoped he couldn't see her lips tremble. Not that it really mattered. He had the gun. "Everyone knows you're the killer."

Yow's laugh sounded more frightening than his threats. "I don't think so. Thomas Goldman is in this so deep all the evidence will point to him."

Mia heard the lack of control in his manic laugh. "Goldman's at the police station."

"He left before you and lover boy did. Stop fooling around and tell me where you stashed that computer. I searched the house and couldn't find it."

"I gave it to the police." Mia tried to stall, "I came back to get my clothes."

Yow stepped closer, and spoke through gritted teeth. "You didn't have it with you on the trail so police don't have it. Now give it to me." He waved the gun threateningly.

Mia tried to think of a way to stall him.

Suddenly a shadow flew out of the corner, and Jake landed on top of Yow. The force of his body knocked the gun out of Yow's hand and both men tumbled to the floor.

Watching helplessly, Mia saw Jake roll on the floor under Yow. But unlike last night on the trail, Jake avoided a blow aimed for his face and escaped Yow's grip. Back on top of his assailant, Jake aimed two swift blows, and knocked Yow out.

Mia rushed to kick the gun out of reach and turned to Jake. "Are you okay?"

"I thought he'd never move far enough into the room so I could jump him." Jake reached her side and too her upper arms in a gentle grip as his gaze warmed her face. "You took too many risks."

"I wanted to hear him talk." Mia stared in Jake's eyes, and wished she could grab hold of him with both hands. "I wanted to hear the details."

"It was risky for me to wait, but once he started talking, he quit moving." Jake pulled her against his chest. "It was a mistake. If he had pulled the trigger—"

"He liked hearing himself talk too much to shoot before he finished bragging."

"Who likes talking now?" Yow demanded from his seat on the floor.

Mia turned in Jake's arms and lost her breath at the sight of Yow sitting upright, aiming the gun at them. She couldn't lose Jake after all this. But Yow rose to his knees, the gun weaving in his hand, ready to shoot.

"Drop the gun and I'll give you the files." She stepped toward Yow.

"Mia, no." Jake grabbed her arm and pulled her behind him. "If you're leaving, Yow, get out now."

"Or what, lover boy? You'll shoot me?" Yow's eyes glowed with unnatural light as he expelled that strange laugh. "Oh, that's right. I have the gun."

Mia moved around Jake on trembling legs. "One thing I don't understand, Mr. Yow. Why kill Leigh Anne Saddler? All the men I talked to loved her. What did you have against her?"

"That cow wouldn't go out with me," Alan Yow snarled as he staggered to his feet. "She slept with all the vice-presidents, but me. When Goldman couldn't get your brother's vote, he sent Leigh Anne to soften him up, because Goldman had doctored the lab results. If the FDA found out, the company would lose millions. Our stock options and pensions would be worthless. We would all be ruined. But Leigh Anne couldn't win your brother's vote. And even after sleeping with him and the others, she wouldn't go out with me."

"That's it?" Mia demanded, unable to believe what he'd said. "You killed Leigh Anne because she wouldn't go out with you?"

Yow shrugged. "That about sums it up. And...I don't have a thing to lose by adding two more bodies to my tally."

Jake lunged forward and knocked the gun out of Yow's hand.

He lifted a hand to slug Yow when the door crashed open. Four police officers in body armor rushed in the room.

Dropping his fist, Jake pushed off Yow and pointed to the gun. One of the officers picked it up. Jake said, "You guys sure took your time."

One of the detectives they'd met at head quarters shoved past the four cops and grinned. "We wanted it all on tape."

Jake mumbled under his breath. "Come on, Mia. Let's get out of here."

"I need my computer." Mia pointed to the sofa. "It's under the couch."

"I need the tape." The detective held out his hand.

Mia stood rigid as he reached in her bra and pulled the recording device out. "I hope this is over, now."

"Not yet." Jake stood up with her laptop in his hands. "I want this to go on record." He stepped close and wrapped his arms around her. "I love you, Mia Clark, but promise me this is the last time you'll play detective. My heart couldn't stand losing you."

"You love me? Really?" Mia smiled wide. "You're not just saying that because I said it first?"

"Being first doesn't matter," Jake leaned down and kissed her, "it's staying in for the whole race that matters. Love me, Mia. Be my wife." Love shown out his eyes as Jake stared at her.

Her heart thumped. "I love you, Jake. I want to be your bride."

"Are we wrapped up, now?" The detective grinned. "I think we're out of tape."

"We're good," Jake stared lovingly into Mia's eyes. "All I need now is time with my future bride."

Mia sighed. "I love you." All her doubts faded away as they walked out of the room. "Can we have the wedding soon?"

"As soon as possible." Jake pulled her in his arms for another kiss.

Dear Reader,

Thank you for reading Flames of Deceit. I hope you enjoyed reading Mia and Jake's story as much as I enjoyed writing it.

The heartbreak of watching the graceful old courthouse go up in flames tore at me until my imagination provided characters to share the pain. Because of the loss...the opposite theme from the trust and loyalty that win the day...both characters needed to have painful memories in their background.

Mia's story isn't tragic as Jake's but a common issue, all the same.

Love, trust and loyalty are words we can all live by...look for them in your life.

If you enjoyed this book, please leave a review.

Happy Reading,

Books by Carol Hutchens:

THE SUBSTITUTE BRIDE   [Redbud Romance #1]
A famous heiress and her actor fiancé want to avoid the media frenzy surrounding their coming wedding so they arrange for substitutes to take their place. When THE SUBSTITUTE BRIDE falls for her groom, the story starts.

A BRIDE FOR MR. RIGHT   [Redbud Romance #2]
Instead of a job using her shiny new degree, the heroine arrives in Redbud shortly after her grandmother's funeral. She inherits her grandmother's house and business. The bookkeeping service doesn't earn enough to pay the bills, but rent on the office is paid for a year so she has to try to turn things around. But sparks fly when our hero returns to town, buys the building and evicts his only tenant, our heroine.

WHERE THE HEART IS   [Redbud Romance #3]
In six short months, Lilly buried both her parents, was downsized from her job, and finds her fiancé in bed with her roommate. Determined to start a new life, Lilly arrives in Redbud to have a baby abandoned in her arms, and learn a famous NASCAR driver is trying to ruin her grandmother's home. And that's just her first

day in town. From that day forth, Trey Lancer gives her headache after the other...and worms his way into her heart.

DR'S SURPRISE TRIPLETS, WIFE NEEDED

A Cinderella romance. But instead of three wicked stepsisters, Cydney Eller has pre-mature triplets left motherless after her sister's accident. The prince is Dr. Daniel Prince who delivers the triplets and demands custody when he learns his brother might be the father. It isn't a glass slipper, but preemie sized diapers and health emergencies that bring these two strangers together to protect three innocent babies. Can love follow?

THE BEST MAN

A second chance at love story. After her husband left her for dead when a tsunami hit their vacation island, Kate Summers returns to reclaim her life. Her return home from the dead is on the same day her husband is standing in church to marry another woman. Kate's attempt to prevent a major legal disaster from happening, throws her right into the arms of THE BEST MAN. Does she dare trust in love a second time?

WHEN A DOG PLAYS CUPID   [Cupid series, Book #1]

A story clipped from the headlines. When one of her patrons at the pet spa dies, naming Kit McFarlan co-guardian of a bad tempered Chihuahua that inherited her millions, fur flies. The woman's nephew, and the co guardian, Drew Webber wants Kit to take charge of the dog. But Kit has secrets. She wants out of the pet business, but her grandmother borrowed money from Drew's aunt. Kit must repay the loan to honor her grandmother's memory, but she can not tolerate the grouchy three pound mutt. Can a nasty tempered 'rat-dog' play cupid for two people needing love?

HERO'S BALL...Cupid Book #2

Can Kit's friend from When A Dog Plays Cupid find her 'real true love' or will her secret new part time job ruin everything? Can the plus sized beautician win a return vet and local firefighting hero's heart of will posing as a model for a plus size catalogue scare him away?

Can a war veteran find the courage to go against his family's wealth and ambitions to make his own way in life? Does a name and position make the man, or does what he believes in stand for something?

Watch for 'Cupid dog's return' when these two face their true desires.

HOW CAN THE HEART FORGET [Medical Conference Cruise]

This is a story of lovers reunited on a Medical Conference Cruise.

Doctors Hart and Stone, together again. Can they forget past mistakes make things right this time? Can her deep longing to have a baby overcome her pain at losing his child? Can his fear of a disease that could destroy his surgical skills, also destroy their chances of sharing their love?

A reunion romance, on a cruise around the Hawaiian Islands, what more could you want?

WHO MURDERED MR. WICKHAM

Only a few months married, Jane Bingley gives her first ball to establish her position in society as Mr. Bingley's wife. Secretly, she hopes to find suitable husbands for her younger sisters and Caroline Bingley. Yet, much as Jane longs to see her beloved family, she worries whether or not Lydia and Mr. Wickham will attend the ball.

Other issues threaten success of the ball, as well, when Jane invites guests staying at Lucas Lodge. Jane is uneasy as to how Lydia and Lizzy will react when Mr. Wickham's former love interest, Miss King, arrives with Sir William and Lady Lucas.

However, none of Jane's fears included a murder occurring at her ball. When the body is discovered, Lydia blames not only Mary King, and the Foresters, but her sister, Lizzy as well. Frantic to salvage the event, Jane convinces Mr. Bingley they must prove none of their family committed the murder, and she gains an unexpected ally in Mary King. However, Miss King is also accused of the crime, and Jane and Mr. Bingley face the possibility of one of their guests being the murderer. Can Jane and Mr. Bingley discover Who Murdered Mr. Wickham before another guest dies?

ABOUT THE AUTHOR

A reader of romance since her early teens, Carol spent many hours doing chores and making up her own romance stories. College brought interesting conflicts, one being whether to major in biology or home economics. Both majors were heavy with science classes but the creative side of home economics won her over.

A teaching career followed, with marriage to her own hero and two wonderful sons. Yet, the stories in her head would not be still. When she retired from teaching, she started putting her dreams on paper and this book is one of the results.

www.ingramcontent.com/pod-product-compliance
Lightning Source LLC
Chambersburg PA
CBHW071235130626

46556CB00003B/1016